FATAL HEAT

Also by Lisa Marie Rice

The Protectors Trilogy
Coming Soon: *Nightfire*
Hotter Than Wildfire
Into the Crossfire

The Dangerous Trilogy
Dangerous Passion
Dangerous Secrets
Dangerous Lover

FATAL HEAT

A SEAL Novella

LISA MARIE RICE

AVONIMPULSE

FATAL HEAT copyright 2011 by Lisa Marie Rice; Excerpt from NIGHTFIRE copyright 2012 by Lisa Marie Rice; Excerpt from INTO THE CROSSFIRE copyright 2010 by Lisa Marie Rice; Excerpt from HOTTER THAN WILDFIRE copyright 2011 by Lisa Marie Rice. All rights reserved under International and Pan-American Copyright Conventions. By payment of the required fees, you have been granted the nonexclusive, nontransferable right to access and read the text of this e-book on-screen. No part of this text may be reproduced, transmitted, downloaded, decompiled, reverse engineered, or stored in or introduced into any information storage and retrieval system, in any form or by any means, whether electronic or mechanical, now known or hereinafter invented, without the express written permission of HarperCollins e-books.

EPub Edition October 2011 ISBN: 9780062115201

Print Edition ISBN: 9780062127549

10 9 8 7 6

FATAL HEAT

CHAPTER ONE

April 2
San Sebastian, California

"That must have hurt like a bitch," a voice said out of the darkness. A female voice. A very sexy female voice. "Here, have a cookie."

Max Wright sat up painfully, shocked out of his funk. Someone lived next door?

Fuck.

He'd assumed he was going to put his broken body back together without anyone watching. His commander had simply handed him the keys to his vacation beach apartment and given him orders to get better. He hadn't said anything about neighbors. Not this early in the season.

Get better.

Those orders still had a bitter taste. Because with a lot of time and a lot of pain and a lot of rehab, he was walking—or, to be honest, limping—again, and he'd gotten back most of his upper-body strength.

But he was out of the navy and no longer a SEAL—permanently. So how was "better" in any way a possibility? Even in the same fucking ballpark of a possibility?

The voice was female. Soft, sympathetic, slightly amused.

He wasn't going to growl, *Yeah, it hurt like a bitch*, even though it had, because pain wasn't important. As every senior chief in the history of the universe screamed, *pain is weakness leaving the body*. Pain was nothing.

He wanted to snarl something but it would be to empty air, because there was a slight click, then a light *woof!* that had him raising his eyebrows, and he was alone.

With a plate of cookies on the tile divider between the two balconies.

Shit. No one to snarl at.

But . . . cookies.

Max had had no appetite since the attack, none. For the first month in ICU, they'd fed him through goddamned tubes bored into his belly, and when they took the tubes out, food tasted like cardboard dipped in shit.

The cookies smelled really good, though. *Really* good. The plate was within reaching distance, and a good thing, too, because getting up and walking at the end of another day in which he'd pushed the limits entailed a cane and a whole lot of pain.

As a matter of fact, the doctors had been adamant that he still needed to stay in the rehab unit for another month, maybe two. He'd had to check himself out, signing his name with a flourish and handing it to the nurse, who clicked her tongue in disapproval.

Tough shit.

Max wanted *out*. He wanted out of this place with all the

sick people. He didn't need reminding he wasn't whole. He knew.

He'd been strong all his life. He knew what he was now. Weak.

He wanted a place that didn't smell of Lysol and Formalin, a place where no one would harp that he was overdoing it, and a place where people didn't smile at him professionally when he was in a shitty mood. Goddamn it, snarl *back*.

It was a good thing they'd taken his guns away in rehab because he'd have ended up shooting someone.

Prison would arguably be worse than the rehab clinic, so before he offed the next smiling sadist, he signed himself out. His XO, Commander Mel Dempsey, offered the use of his vacation beach house about half an hour north of Monterey, handing him the keys and telling him to get better.

It was off-season. Max wanted peace and quiet and solitude while he put himself back together again.

He didn't want next-door neighbors, female or otherwise. He liked women as much as the next man, maybe more, but not now. Not while he threw up if he moved too fast, not while one leg wouldn't bear his full weight, not while he was this pathetic . . . fucking . . . *cripple*.

Cookie Lady had a real sexy voice, and the very little he'd seen of her in the dim light—wow. But he wasn't coming out to play. Not for a long while.

He was going to eat what he could choke down, sleep as well as he could, pump iron, do the exercises the rehab doc had given him, and walk along the beach, making sure he didn't fall on his ass. All those good things. And keep his dick down.

Not hard to do.

His dick had disappeared after surgery. Oh, it was physically there, all right. Mainly as a tube to piss through. Not even a twinge of sex, not even with the nurses in the hospital. Not even with Nurse Carrie, who'd looked really hot in white and had offered.

Max didn't want any. He didn't want anything at all except to get back on his feet and back in the Teams.

Not going to happen.

He didn't want pity or commiseration, he wanted to be left fucking *alone*.

Though, actually, the neighbor lady had left him alone. With cookies.

Goddamn it, who the fuck left cookies for a SEAL? SEALs ate rocks and shat nails. They didn't eat fucking cookies. They—

A stray gust of wind blew from the sea and he froze.

Damn, those cookies smelled good.

He had long arms. He didn't have to get up. He held a cookie up in the dim light and bit in.

Best cookies he'd ever had, bar none. White chocolate chip. Perfect cookie in a world of imperfection.

He sat and glowered at the dark sea and ate the plateful up.

In his dreams, it was always the same and always different.

He was in Helmand: the desolate dun-colored peaks of the Hindu Kush rising sharp and jagged around him, the air so clear his binocs showed him the valley floor as clearly as if it were ten feet away instead of a thousand.

He saw everything with crystal clarity.

It was a mission to take out a real bad guy, Ahmed Sahar. A warlord who'd become Al Qaida's go-to guy and was funnelling arms to the Taliban. Also a world-class crazy. A fucking psychopath.

From his hilltop sniper's den, Max had watched two executions and the lashing of a young girl. He couldn't wait to have the fucker in his crosshairs. Sahar was a psychopath—but a crafty one—and stayed in his compound year-round. But they had intel that a major operation was in the works and Sahar would have to travel.

Max had been waiting for three days in his hideSTET under netting, pissing in a bottle, never sleeping, barely breathing. Because he really, *really* wanted to nail the fucker.

And—there he was! Coming out of the gates, looking around for his enemies. *Up here, fuckhead,* Max thought, finger loose on the trigger.

It was a convoy, but Sahar wanted to oversee something, and got out of his vehicle to shout at the lead driver. Max kept him in the sights: that gross, misshapen head he'd studied for hours while being briefed.

This was it. Sahar straightened and took one last look around as Max let out half a breath and gently squeezed the trigger. Sahar's head exploded. A swift clean head shot.

His work here was done.

Except when the bullet pulped Sahar's head, *another* crazy shouldered a long tube. Someone had told Max—who was really good with guns, who had shot maybe a million rounds in his life—that some Afghanis had a mystical relationship with arms. Max believed it, because though Second Psychopath couldn't have had a clue where the supersonic bullet came from—and it would take a team of forensic experts hours to ascertain the direction of the shot—Second Psychopath had no problems.

Second Psychopath's head swivelled and in one second he somehow nailed Max's position. Max watched as the tube foreshortened and Second Psychopath was rocked back on his sandals, something trailing a cloud of smoke spearing its way to him.

The world exploded in fire and pain . . .

Max bolted up, panting, twisted in sweat-soaked sheets, teeth clenched hard against any possible sound, the way he always woke up from his nightmares. The legacy of a childhood spent terrified of waking up his stepfather, who plunged into terrifying rages at the slightest provocation.

Nightmares without noise were his special gift, learned before he could talk.

But even without noise, they left him sweaty and drained and shaking. He hated it, hated them.

He slipped out of bed, lurched once on his bad leg, and caught himself.

Getting strong again would help. Being strong and staying strong had always been his touchstone, was the reason he'd survived his childhood. That was how he'd got his Budweiser. That and being too damned stubborn to quit.

Losing his strength after the RPG attack had been the hardest thing in a hard life.

Mel had a fully-equipped gym in the garage, but even if it weren't there, Max would have improvised one. Plastic bags or empty milk bottles filled with sand, fingertip pull-ups from the door frame, a two-by-four as an ab bench—he'd done it all as a kid.

Time to sweat out the nightmare. When he walked into the gym with its gleaming equipment, the sky outside the window was slate gray. An hour later, wiping the sweat from his chest, it was pearl gray.

The ocean was forty feet away. Back in the day, forty feet was laughable, nothing. He could run it in a few seconds. He ran ten miles a day in boots, every day, and did a hundred push-ups at the end of the run. He didn't do it laughing, but he did it.

No running now. Maybe not ever. His doctors had originally said he'd never walk again and now look at him. Of course he didn't walk so much as lurch. Each step took a second and sent a wire of pain straight into his head.

But in the water . . . ah, in the water he was still a god. An injured god, slower than any of his Team mates, but still faster than most civilians.

Time to swim. He looked forward to his long daily swims where his mangled leg was merely a deadweight. Slipping into the water was a delight. He headed out into the still-dark ocean with strong, sure strokes, using his arms more than his legs, the sun sliding up into the sky at his back.

If he'd had the ocean a few steps away a year ago when he'd woken up from surgery, as soon as he could walk he'd have been tempted to swim as far as his strength could carry him—so far he could never make it back—and die a swimmer's death.

Better than the death that was staring him in the face: pissing into a bag, needing help to sip soup. If he'd had the means and the strength to end it those first few months, he would have. But they'd watched over him and nothing sharp was ever within reach.

And so he determined that he'd walk again and, by God, inch by trembling inch he'd done it. The physical therapist threatened to tie him down because he did too much, but he knew his own body. His body wanted to stand upright, wanted the challenge. Going slow was not an option.

He swam for an hour until his strength began to fail. He'd gone less than a mile. He hated that. During BUD/S he'd swim five miles, come out of the surf running, hit the grinder to pound out a hundred push-ups. Now he was exhausted as he trod water.

There was a small island three miles out. Some kind of research facility, his XO had told him. Santo Domingo Island. Goddamn it, he was going to get to the point where he could swim there and back, no matter what it took.

The swim back was slow, his muscles not pulling him smoothly and strongly through the water as they were supposed to. He started trembling.

Fuck this. It didn't matter that he wasn't even supposed to be upright. That the doctors had told him he might never walk again. He was a fucking SEAL. And SEALs didn't do weakness.

He dove under, swimming the last fifty yards under water, knowing he couldn't possibly do a hundred push-ups at the end.

Max strained toward shore, fighting the urge to breathe, at the very limit of his strength, when he suddenly heard his name called. A female voice, calling his name.

What the fuck? A mermaid? Some kind of underwater creature calling him down to his death?

He reared up from the water.

And something strong and hairy, moving fast, cannon-balled into him, taking him back under before he had a chance to fill his lungs with air.

Oh no!

Paige Waring stepped back in dismay. A man had suddenly appeared out of the water, rising up like some mythic sea god. Max jumped him and he tumbled back under.

Her gorgeous, smart, totally undisciplined dog Max, who growled at some men and became instant best friends with others.

The man he'd jumped was so frightening-looking she couldn't understand Max's friendliness.

He looked like he'd eat you for breakfast and spit out the bones. And he was her new neighbor.

She'd known only that her new neighbor was a former naval officer recovering from wounds sustained in combat. Though Uncle Mel hadn't said it, she supposed her new neighbor was a SEAL, because that's what Uncle Mel was.

The man crested the surface, Max jumping and yapping happily around him.

He didn't look frightening—he looked terrifying. Last night she'd had the impression in the darkness of danger on a hair trigger.

A wounded officer next door. She was hardwired to try to do something for him. After all, he'd been wounded in the service of his country. So she'd baked cookies, meaning to go over and invite him to a glass of wine and cookies as a neighborly gesture.

Then she'd seen him, a huge figure in the semi-darkness, face grim and frightening. One leg extended, thinner than the other one, which was thick with muscle. The damaged leg had looked so mangled and scarred, it hurt to look at it.

He'd turned to her, and even in the gloom his face was frightening, speaking of the terrible things he'd seen. The terrible things that had been done to him.

She'd murmured a few words, left the cookies on the balcony between them, and retreated to her apartment because the guy sitting out there in the dark didn't look like a nice neighbor. He looked like a killer.

Now he rose back up from the waves, water streaming off him. And up and up. He was tall and huge. Or had been huge. He was on the thin side, but he had the bones of a big man: broad-shouldered, long-legged, with enormous hands.

Crisscrossed with scars. Terrible scars. Life-threatening scars. On top of that mangled leg.

Paige stood and stared. He seemed like a creature from the mists of time, a ravaged warrior misplaced on their tame stretch of beach.

Max jumped him again and Paige broke out of the spell she'd been under. She had to save her dog. This man could hurt Max badly with one swipe of one of those enormous hands.

"Down, Max, down!" she cried, rushing forward into the surf, heart pounding. She was ready to face the man down to defend her dog, but heavens, he looked terrifying.

Max leaped again and she saw the man's weight shift to that mangled leg, and he faltered.

"Max!" Paige clapped her hands because a dog instructor—one of the many to whom she'd taken her loveable but absolutely incorrigible dog—had told her it was a signal for dogs to calm down.

Not Max—he was rollicking in the waves, jumping on the man.

The man made a gesture with his big hand, and to her astonishment, Max settled a little, dropping his front paws back into the sea.

The skin on his back rippled and Paige's eyes widened.

"No!" she shouted.

But it was too late. Max shook all over, drenching her and the man. He was wet all over anyway, but she'd have to shower again before heading to work.

Oh God. Max had knocked this man down and showered him with doggy-smelling seawater. Who knew how he would react?

And then the man looked at her and grinned. It was a mere flash, a movement of the edges of his mouth, a glimpse of white teeth, and then his face settled back into its usual grim lines.

"Cookie Lady," he said. "The cookies were great."

His voice was unusually deep and dark, completely out of place on this bright sunny morning. She shivered.

"Yes. Cookie Lady." She looked at him—at the height of him, the breadth of him, that face that was now totally unsmiling. It had to be done. She was in the wrong. Her dog had made a man with a crippled leg tumble into the ocean.

So she did the brave thing and offered her hand. Hoping he wouldn't notice that it trembled. Hoping he'd give it back unharmed.

Paige disliked shaking hands with macho men. She needed her hands to do delicate lab work. Often guys felt they had to prove their manhood with their grip. This one looked like he could crush her hand with no effort at all.

But . . . her dog *had* jumped him. And Uncle Mel was his commanding officer.

"I'm really, really sorry. I'd like to say that I don't know what got into my dog, but he's always like this. I seem to spend all my time apologizing for him. I'm Paige. Paige Waring."

His hand enveloped hers in a strong, gentle grip. His hand felt like warm steel. He might be wounded, but his grip was like touching a live wire, crackling with electricity. She was so surprised, she kept her hand in his as if the electricity had created some kind of chemical bond.

"Max."

At hearing his name, Max gave a happy bark and jumped both of them. Paige lost her footing in the surf and would have fallen if he hadn't immediately snaked a big arm around her, pulling her upright and against him in an unshakeable grasp.

His leg might be mangled and he might be overly thin, but there was no mistaking the strength in the muscles she found herself plastered against.

It was intensely embarrassing and—whoa—incredibly exciting. The only other man who looked this strong was Uncle Mel, but she'd never been in a full frontal embrace with him.

She'd never felt a man this strong before.

Her father, bless his soul, had been thin and stoop-shouldered, and was undoubtedly right this minute leafing through ancient history texts in heaven. And the men she dated were mainly fellow scientists. Nice guys, but nerds mostly.

Nothing like this. Nothing at all.

Even though he'd been in the chilly Pacific, he radiated

heat and a very male kind of electricity she'd never encountered before but recognized instantly, as if a hundred years of female empowerment and her PhD had been suddenly stripped away, leaving a breathless female reacting to an alpha male.

He was reacting, too, the merest hint of a stirring against her belly when Max barked and jumped them again.

Paige moved away, lifting Max's paws off them. "Down, boy," she chided. "*Down.*" Looking up, she caught a fleeting expression cross his face, his eyes flaring. It was over so quickly she wondered whether she'd imagined the whole thing. But in the meantime, her pulse quickened and her mouth went dry.

This was ridiculous and very unlike her.

He was a neighbor—a wounded soldier, formerly under the command of her godfather—and he'd been jumped by her dog. He deserved better than a hormone-stricken woman rendered breathless by beefcake.

She straightened, tilting her head back to look him straight in the eyes. Dark brown, very intense eyes. And highly intelligent ones, too. That shook her for a moment. She was totally unused to male intelligence as a subset of muscle.

Mostly, in her experience, male intelligence was linked to white lab coats. Definitely not huge expanses of tough, naked, tanned skin.

"I'm really sorry, Lieutenant—"

"Max," he said, and her dog woofed.

Why was he—oh! "Your name is Max, too?"

"Like your dog." He dipped his head, her hand still in his. "Maxwell Wright. Max for short."

"He's Maximilian. Max for short."

She tugged and he let go of her hand. It felt like she'd

been unplugged from some arcane power source. "Lieutenant Wright." That had been the name Uncle Mel had said.

Another expression crossed his face. Not of heat and amusement, but of grief. Deep, painful grief. She'd just lost her father. She understood grief, understood it in her bones.

"Not lieutenant," he said. "Not anymore."

Involuntarily, Paige looked down at his leg. With that leg—much thinner than the other one, crisscrossed with scars—he wouldn't be an acting naval officer, no. One leg was brown and powerful, thickly muscled—the other pale, the muscles withered.

And all those other scars. Surgical scars, mostly, white lines with tiny tucks on each side, crisscrossing his chest. One round puckered scar in his shoulder, which even she could see was a gunshot wound, looked to be older than the others.

Her dog looked from one to the other while they were talking, brown eyes trained on his mistress and on his new best friend. He obviously decided all this talking was boring, and he hunched his shoulders, which is what he did before leaping.

Paige gasped. The other Max, the human one, was going to get jumped again, knocked down again. "Max, no! Bad boy!"

It was perfectly pointless because Max never obeyed. She stooped to grab ahold of his collar when human Max made another slight gesture with one big hand, and her Max relaxed.

Amazing.

Then she looked up again at the big man and realized just why Max had rethought his Jumping on Everyone is Fun philosophy. The man had "command" written all over him, just as Uncle Mel had. It was unthinkable that anyone, man or beast, would not obey him instantly.

It must be a great trait to have, one she sadly lacked.

Her Max whined, looking back and forth between them.

Human Max scratched Max's head, never averting his gaze from hers. It was unnerving, being watched so closely, particularly by a man who managed to project such a forceful personality even standing barefoot in the surf dressed only in swim trunks.

Maybe it was all those muscles.

She had to go. Though she felt almost mesmerized by the tall, silent, unsmiling man in front of her, she was going to be late for work if she stood around much longer, mooning over broad shoulders and an ability to hypnotize her notoriously unruly dog into a semblance of obedience.

"So. Um . . ." God. His eyes were so dark, so compelling . . . she almost stuck her hand out simply to feel that electric connection again. But that would be crazy.

Paige wasn't crazy. She was a staid scientist, normally totally immune to hormonal urges like wanting to hold a man's strong hand after a few moments' acquaintance. Max lifted a paw to her thigh, wetting her sundress. Time to go. "I'm really sorry my dog jumped you, um, lieutenant."

"Max," he said, his voice so deep she was surprised the water they were in didn't vibrate.

"Max," she repeated obediently. She tugged at her Max's leash. "I try to train him, but as you can see, I'm not very successful. He wasn't born with the obedience gene." She shot a wry glance down at the dog by her side. Alas, Max wasn't quelled at all to hear his faults described. His brown and tan tail wagged so fast it shot off drops of salt water.

"What is he? Looks like some border collie in there." The

man's big hand was scratching behind Max's ears. Max knew they were talking about him, and his rump now moved together with his tail. He was in dog heaven.

She sighed. "He's a rescue and he's a mix. Some border collie, sure. The guy at the pound said there was also some Labrador and German shepherd, too. He all but *promised* me that Max was bred for decorum and obedience." With hindsight, Paige was astonished that a lightning bolt hadn't shot down out of the sky to strike dead that helpful college student at the pound.

Her dog grinned, tongue lolling out of his mouth, perfectly aware of the fact that neither decorum nor obedience was high on his list of doggy priorities.

"Come on, big guy." Paige nodded to her dog. "Walk's over. Time to go back home. I have to go to work. Some of us work for a living, you know."

Her dog was very smart and had learned quite a few words. Pity *stay*, *heel*, and *sit* weren't among them. But *work*, which meant she was leaving him locked up in her tiny backyard all day—well, he understood that word just fine.

Max had perfected the art of emotional blackmail. The instant he heard the word *work*, he cowered, whining. Big brown eyes looked up beseechingly.

Paige barely kept from rolling her eyes. She looked up at the tall dark man at her side. He wasn't smiling, not exactly. But his features had lightened.

"You're probably thinking that I regularly take the whip to him, the way he's reacting, when actually he's spoiled to death. If it were up to him, my main job would be taking him for endless walks and feeding him. 24/7. But the fact is," she switched her attention to her whining dog, raising her voice, "the fact is I've got a day job, which is what keeps *someone* in *treats*."

That was another word he recognized. He greeted it with a happy bark.

She turned back to the tall soldier. "So, I apologize again for my unruly dog, and now we'll get out of your hair." She tugged at the leash and Max did his usual cowering act, as if she were the Angel of Death come to smite him. "Come on, Max. Playtime's over." She tugged again, walking backwards. Sometimes she had to literally drag him away from the beach, his paws leaving tracks in the sand. She'd gotten quite a few dirty looks from that.

"He can stay with me." The voice was low but his words carried.

"I beg your pardon?"

"He clearly doesn't want to be locked up, not quite yet. And I—I have some free time. I'd be happy to take him for another walk. Keep him on the beach for a while longer."

She couldn't help herself. She looked down at that scarred leg. When she looked back up at him, she saw calm in those dark eyes.

"He won't make me fall. I have good balance. He caught me by surprise but it won't happen again."

"I don't know . . . he doesn't tire easily," she warned.

That earned her a small smile. "Neither do I."

Well, no. If he'd been a Navy SEAL he could probably outlast her rambunctious dog.

She looked at him carefully, not in any way hiding her scrutiny. He stood still for it, face remote and expressionless, and let her examine him.

Paige had no idea who he was, really. Though she complained often about Max's rambunctiousness and complete lack of obedience, he was a joy. On days when work was going badly, which was happening more and more often lately, coming home to Max was the one bright spot in her day.

She loved him fiercely.

Though Max was a friendly dog, he'd had several unexpectedly hostile reactions to men. One, a colleague, had turned out to be a wife beater; another, a drunk; and one notable evening, he'd growled at a perfectly normal banker who'd come to pick her up for dinner. Max's acumen was better than her own because it took her an entire dinner to realize the banker was a jerk. When he took her home, he wouldn't take no for an answer, and it was only when Max growled—showing sharp, white teeth—that he had backed off.

So she trusted Max's reactions and what she was seeing now was trust and liking. His mouth was open in one of his exasperating, slobbering grins as he watched the dynamic between her and the human Max, tail wagging furiously.

He was actually closer to human Max than to her because though the man was standing utterly still, one hand was still scratching behind Max's ears.

Small Max was a slut for attention, but he wouldn't be reacting this way if Big Max were giving off bad human vibes.

"He's very important to me," she said finally, still watching the man's deep brown eyes, unwavering and intelligent.

His head dipped. "Understood. He'll be safe with me." Max gave a sharp, happy bark. Her dog couldn't possibly know what they were discussing but as far as he was concerned, every minute not spent in her tiny backyard and in the presence of his mistress and a new best friend was a happy minute.

Paige sighed. The decision was made, she was just stalling.

"OK." She handed him the walking-with-Max equipment. Leash. Something less fun than the leash. "That's the pooper-scooper." She eyed him suspiciously. "You know how it works?"

He turned it over in his hands, biting his lips against what looked like a smile. "No, but it looks pretty straightforward. I think I can figure it out."

She glanced at her watch and winced. Ouch. She had to hurry if she was going to be at work on time. Plus she was hoping for Silvia's call. "I'll meet you at your door in twenty minutes and hand you Max's food bowls, some dog food, and a Milk Bone." Max barked at the sound of his favourite words of all time. "If you give me your cell number I'll program it into my cell and I'll give you my number when I bring you Max's stuff, so you can call if anything happens."

"You can give it to me now," he said.

He was naked except for swim trunks. "But you don't have your cell with you."

"I can remember a ten-digit number. Trust me."

She gave him her number and, sure enough, he repeated it back to her perfectly. Whatever his wounds were, they certainly hadn't damaged his brain.

He could contact her if Max got to be too much of a handful. And she had to give him a fallback option. "I'll give you the key to my backyard when I stop by. If you get tired of him, just open the gate and make him walk through. He'll drag his feet and look heartsick, but just ignore him." She gave her dog a quelling look which he happily ignored. Some slobber fell to the sand. "He can get really annoying."

The man went very still. "You don't know me and you're going to give me the key to your backyard?"

Paige smiled. "First of all, I'm leaving you Max, and he is much more precious to me than the backyard I'm too busy to care for, and where Max digs up all the plants anyway. There's nothing there to steal, not even flowers. And Uncle Mel sent you here. My godfather. Uncle Mel more or less walks on water as far as I'm concerned. If you were a serial killer, he'd have let me know."

His face had turned somber. "Not a serial killer, promise."

If he *was* a serial killer, he was a lonely one. Paige recognized loneliness and she was seeing it right in front of her. He was so lonely, even the company of her wildly rambunctious dog was welcome.

"Okay," she said softly. "I'll drop the things off and I'll see you tonight. And as a thank-you for taking care of my dog, I'll even cook you dinner."

Dinner was definitely a word Max recognized. He gave an excited bark.

"I second the motion," the other Max said in his deep, sexy voice.

CHAPTER TWO

M**an, Cookie Lady was fucking** *gorgeous.*

Max was really glad he'd seen her first on the beach, loose and relaxed, because when she stopped by to leave keys and food for the dog, she was all wrapped up tightly in Corporate Woman gear and seemed another woman entirely.

That luscious golden-brown hair pulled back tightly into a French braid. Conservative dark suit. Sensible shoes. Briefcase. Glasses. Nothing at all like the laughing woman in a sundress and sandals, hair loose around her shoulders, playing with her dog.

She had pulled a reverse Marian the Librarian, buttoning up, but it was too late because Max had already seen the skimpy-sundress, bare-legs, hair-down, glasses-off version, and it was stunning.

Noticing women was something new. In the Sandbox and after getting blown up, and while being put back together again, he hadn't desired anyone. There wasn't anyone to desire in the field, and in the hospital, man, you do *not* get a hard-on for the lady who cleans your bedpan and wipes your butt.

And besides, this past year, not much was working south of the border, including his legs.

But his legs—or one leg, at least—were now working, and everything else came back online, in one big rush this morning. On a beach. While wearing swim trunks that outlined him just fine.

Shit, that was close. Standing there in the surf with this beautiful, laughing woman who was trying and failing to show contrition for her dog—so close he could smell something flowery over the brine of the ocean, so close he could see the green flecks in her blue eyes, so close he could touch that clear, lightly-tanned skin . . . he had to curl his hands into fists.

Not reaching out and touching her? Well, it took a SEAL's self-discipline. Because what he wanted more than anything was to go with the rush of hormones suddenly flooding his system. Pull her down in the gently whooshing early-morning surf and roll right on top of her.

He could feel it, he could almost taste it. Just pulling her down with him, lifting that light skirt, hand smoothing up her thighs, ripping off her panties and losing them in the surf, putting his hand between her legs . . .

His long-dormant dick had lengthened and thickened and was well on its way to rising, ready to celebrate breaking its two-year dry spell. He had to will all the blood that had gone AWOL from his head to scramble down to his cock all the way back up, so he could make rational conversation with her without scaring her off.

He hadn't had sex in so long, the desire was as intense as when he'd been a kid with a perpetual hard-on. Hot desire prickled in his veins, made his hands tingle, and filled his chest with heat.

But when he'd been a randy teenager, just about any female who didn't make you run screaming from her—and who had the right plumbing—would do.

This time those intense feelings were focused tightly on *her*. Paige Waring. Cookie Lady. Mistress of Max. Pretty and laughing and luscious.

And then the kicker. A real shock. An invitation to dinner! And sex afterward!

It had been like a punch to the chest, even though the small part of his brain that was still capable of rational thought realized that a dinner invitation wasn't an invitation to sex. That was just dickful thinking.

It was a pity invite. For the crippled soldier, all alone.

Didn't matter.

He didn't feel like a crippled soldier now. Now he felt like a man with a mission. To get the delectable Paige Waring into his bed just as fast as was humanly possible. And since there wasn't a limit on his time because he wasn't on active duty anymore— his heart gave its usual sharp pump at the thought—he was going to keep her there a long, long time. Because man, sex was *back*. Big time.

The dog tugged at his leash, dancing in the waves. He wanted to play.

Well, so did Max. After two years of misery and pain, he was ready to play again.

It was hard to keep Max out of her mind. The human Max, Maxwell—not her furry friend.

Paige had an incredibly frustrating day, trying to piece together corrupted research files from the Argentina Research Station and waiting for her friend Silvia, who worked there, to contact her.

The Argentina research project was interesting, and a little creepy. As a plant geneticist, Paige was fascinated by what nature could do all on its own. But now her company, GenPlant Laboratories—an offshoot of a major food multinational— had spliced a human growth hormone gene into corn, creating a new variety, HGHM-1, intending to produce a type of corn that grew so quickly you could have three crops a year, each crop double the tonnage.

Their research fields were in a vast company landholding four hundred miles south of Buenos Aires and one of her best friends, Silvia Ramirez, was the local project leader.

They'd been playing phone tag for days. Silvia had sent a file of preliminary results, but the file had somehow become corrupted, almost impossible to reconstitute.

Without the files and without Silvia to help her, Paige was stymied. HGHM-1 was the company's top priority at the moment, and she didn't have any other urgent projects which needed her attention.

So Paige spent all day with basically nothing to do but think of her new neighbor. Not obsessing really. Just . . . thinking about him.

He was in pain. He suppressed winces when he put too

much weight on that thin, mutilated leg, but she could tell it hurt him.

He hadn't said a word about it, though, pretending absolutely nothing was wrong. In fact, offered to look after her dog.

It was been a real surprise to her when she opened her mouth to say "no" and "yes" had plopped out.

Much as her Max exasperated her, she loved her dog. The only time she left him with strangers was when she had to leave town on a business trip, and then only at the certified kennel she'd carefully checked over.

So telling a man she didn't know that she'd leave her dog with him for the day was way out of character.

The thing was, for a second there, human Max had looked so lost and lonely. The best remedy for that was time spent with her Max. Her Max would run you ragged chasing after him and keep you laughing all the while. No time to feel lonely. Max was joy incarnate.

The other Max wouldn't be lonely for long, though, once he put himself back together. There was a whole world of women out there who'd love to play with him.

The man simply exuded sex. It came out of his pores. She wondered whether her Max could smell the pheromones coming off him, though maybe males didn't notice hormones from the same gender.

It was an interesting thought.

When Max caught her just before she stumbled into the surf, it had been like receiving an electrical charge. For a second there, she thought she could actually hear electricity crackling, though probably what she heard were her neurons frying. Held tightly against that super-hard, overly lean body really messed with her system. If she'd been one of her test plants, she'd have wilted from overload.

Certainly her brain had left her body. It was already crazy that she'd let him keep Max for the day.

Of course, the man was a naval officer, used to enormous responsibility. He was a SEAL. Or a former SEAL. Those men knew how to do everything, and she was sure he could ride herd over an undisciplined but friendly dog.

Asking him to dinner? Well, that had been a little loony. Not her style at all. She was pretty cool around men. She couldn't remember ever asking a guy out on a date.

Not that the dinner was a *date*, of course. It wasn't, not at all. It was just a friendly neighborly gesture. A thank-you dinner. But once she'd had time to think—to overthink it, Silvia would have said—she realized she'd gone way out of her comfort zone.

She would have called him to cancel, except . . . well, except there was a part of her that looked forward to tonight. That wondered whether the zing she'd felt when she touched him was an outlier.

If she were to plot her emotional reaction to men on x and y axes, the line would wander gently over the lower third of the page. That one experience had been, literally, off the charts. Zipping up to the top and disappearing into the stratosphere.

Her cell phone rang. She snatched it up, hoping it was finally Silvia, and heard static.

Then, faintly, "Paige?" Silvia, sounding as if calling from the back side of the moon. "—Sent you—"

Paige clutched the receiver. "Silvia! Finally! The data file you sent—"

But she was talking to empty air. They'd been disconnected. Again. Paige flipped her cell closed with a frown. Silvia wasn't answering emails, was never online according to Skype, she wasn't Twittering, and her Facebook page hadn't been updated—something she did at least three times a week.

Silvia, the most gregarious person Paige knew, seemed to have dropped off the face of the earth. She would never leave Paige wondering where she was. If Silvia were capable of getting in touch, Paige knew, she would.

And the file she sent had been hacked and corrupted. Paige was sure of it. But who to complain to? Silvia's attachment had been personal, not part of the regular updates of the Argentina Research Station's reports to the head office. Officially, the attachment didn't exist.

Well, this had been an unproductive day. Worrying about Silvia and mooning over her next-door neighbor.

She hung up her lab coat, unbraided her hair—her own personal signal for being off-duty—and walked out the big two-story glass doors of the research complex.

Worry drummed in her heart. For her friend, and because she had a file-restoration app a lovesick nerd had once designed for her in grad school, in the hope of luring Paige into his bed. The ruse hadn't worked but the app did.

It looked like the file had been degraded by a pro, but Nerd-App had restored bits and pieces. One sentence had leaped out at her, chilling her to the core.

Strong evidence of a human carcino—

The sentence was incomplete, but the only word in the English language that began with those letters was "carcinogen."

Something in what Silvia was studying was giving humans cancer. And Silvia was nowhere to be found.

There was absolutely nothing Paige could do, not at the moment. The head of her department, Dr. Warren Beaverton, was in Estonia for a conference. And though Dr. Beaverton was excellent at what he did, outside generating lab data he was a useless human being with barely enough backbone to stand up straight.

And right above him was Vice President for Research Dean Hyland, who, on a scale of humanity, one to ten, ranked minus-five. And who, being corporate, knew less than her cleaning lady about genetics. She had no idea how he'd gotten his degree. Bought it, probably, from some online company based in Montenegro.

Instinctively, Paige knew she couldn't involve either one.

Something was really wrong. At times, when Paige lifted her extension, there was a slight humming sound before the click of connection.

She didn't have to read thrillers to know what that meant. Her phone and undoubtedly her office computer were being watched. It would take nothing to tempest her keyboard so they could follow stroke by stroke what she wrote.

Silvia was smart and so was she. If they could just communicate briefly, they could figure out a way to talk without being overheard. They could set up a message board, they could invent new Skype names, they could communicate via throwaway cells.

But first, Paige had to be able to talk to Silvia.

And Silvia was nowhere to be found.

At least she had the two Maxes tonight to take her mind off her worries.

Chapter Three

Max stood on the doorstep, trying to keep his jaw from dropping, drinking in the sight of Paige in the open doorway. This was the third version of Paige Waring he'd seen, and if the first two bowled him over, this one took his breath away. *Kapow!* Dead man standing.

The laughing beachcomber and staid businesswoman were gone. In their place was this sexy knockout.

That shiny, light brown hair—enough for about six women—shimmered around her shoulders, reflecting the light with every move she made.

She'd put makeup on that highlighted her large blue-green eyes and made that lush mouth a work of art. She had on a simple, elegant, sexy, frothy turquoise summer dress, white and turquoise bangles, and open-toed sandals showing bright pink toenails. Even her fucking *toes* were sexy.

A stronger version of the perfume he'd smelled this morning mixed with warm skin would have brought him to his knees—if he were able to bend both knees.

She was a wet dream come to life, she lived right next door, and she was about to feed him.

Max leaned down to unleash the dog and to give him time to hide his reaction, because staring slack-jawed at a woman was definitely uncool.

The instant the snap of the leash was undone, the dog bounded forward. He was crazy-eager to get to his mistress, though Max had learned today that crazy-eager was the dog's default setting. He'd been crazy-eager to chase squirrels in the small, dog-friendly park at the far end of the beach, he'd been crazy-eager to play Frisbee on the sand, he'd been crazy-eager to play fetch with a stick in the surf.

He was crazy-eager about everything, and keeping him out of trouble had kept Max on the move and in a good mood all day.

Max jumped his mistress, trying to reach her face and lick it. Paige stepped back, almost falling under the dog's weight.

Max snapped out of his Paige-trance.

"Max!" He put command in his voice. "Sit!"

Immediately, Max plopped his butt on the floor. The discipline lasted a second as he shivered with excitement, then hind muscles bunched for another leap on Paige.

"Stay!" Max commanded, and surreptitiously slipped him a doggie treat. He'd never thought to try that with his men. Give them a command, then slip them a Mars bar when they obeyed.

Now it was Paige's pretty jaw that dropped. She gazed wide-eyed down at her dog then up at him. "Oh my gosh! He obeyed you! That's amazing, how did you manage that?" She narrowed her eyes at him. "And don't you dare say it's because you're a man."

He clenched his jaw closed because, well, it was true. He was used to commanding men. Corralling her dog into something resembling discipline came easily to him.

"I won't say that. Promise." Max wasn't a fool. He wanted to keep on her good side. "Here." He pulled his hand from behind his back to show her a bouquet of flowers. "Believe it or not, your dog picked them out. He sniffed at all the florist's bouquets and decided on this one. Just sat down in front of it and wouldn't budge until I bought it. I have no idea what the flowers are."

She was smiling as she took the bouquet, sniffing appreciatively. "Thanks, though it wasn't necessary. Let's see, we have black-eyed Susans, African daisies, Gladioli, Zinnias and Asters."

His eyebrows rose. "That's impressive. I know daisies from roses, but that's about it. I know edible mushrooms and those that will poison you." And how to make deadly oleander tea.

"Don't be too impressed," Paige called out as she walked into a small, pretty, light-filled kitchen and came back out with a vase. "Knowing plants is my job. I'm a plant geneticist." She looked at his face and laughed. "I get that blank look a lot. No one knows what to say to that. Must be like your line of work. Come on in and sit down; can I serve you a glass of wine?"

The dog was whining and wriggling at his feet. Max looked at Paige. "Thanks. I'd love a glass of wine. What are we going to do about Max? I think we've reached the limits of my one-day training course."

Paige turned back to the kitchen, her words trailing. "Well, I do happen to have some *treats* for a *good dog*." As if the words were a trigger releasing a spring, Max leaped up and scrambled into the kitchen, nails clicking madly on the tile floor.

Well, it was good while it lasted. No one could expect a dog barely out of puppyhood to stay still forever. Particularly after only one day of training.

Max was jumping up and down, making light yips of joy. Paige bent down open-handed, and he ate the treats delicately from her palm, then licked it. Paige laughed and ruffled the fur on the top of his head as he looked up at her adoringly.

Max understood perfectly. The instant he'd seen Paige on the doorstep, so pretty and smiling, something in him—something painful and dark and twisted—cracked open, just a little.

Amazing.

The groundwork had been laid by a sunny day with an energetic, affectionate dog, and now the work was complete in the presence of its mistress.

Paige exuded calm. Sexy, radiant serenity. Did such a thing exist? Hell if he knew. But if it did, she had it in spades.

The way she moved, those luscious yet slender curves, some kind of perfume that moved straight into a man's nose and zapped the thinking part of his brain—those were there. But there was also some kind of serene force field around her. She moved in her pretty orderly space like some kind of angel sent to earth to remind him that life was good, was worth living. That life wasn't battle and death and loss. Blood and pain. That life had things that were worth fighting for.

Paige and her funny, hyperactive dog—hell, yes, they were worth fighting for. What he was watching was a scene that was unthinkable in certain parts of the world. A serene, successful, single woman who lived alone with a dog.

Where he'd spent the last years of his career, right now a woman like Paige would be lashed and then stoned, her dog whipped and despised.

He was really glad he'd worked so hard to create a world where that kind of horrific cruelty could be defeated. He didn't regret anything. Particularly not now, in this light-filled room with a beautiful, smiling woman.

There was just something about her. The world needed women just like her. Needed women who could make things better just by being.

And right there, in Paige's colorful kitchen—sipping a glass of excellent chilled white wine with Her dog dancing around her feet, watching her move so gracefully—something happened to Max.

He'd spent years in very bad places. Culminating in that last year in Afghanistan, which broke his heart and his body. And then the hospital, lashed to the bed by pain and weakness. Dark years, years with feral beings around him, years feeling that the world was hung together with fraying ropes and fraying hopes.

Right now, right this moment, watching the evening light flood the pretty apartment, something powerful moved through him, some force that was strong enough to shift the darkness in him that was heavy as iron, hard as rock. Something made of light, intangible yet very real, very strong.

Whatever it was, it was intimately connected with the beautiful woman humming to a tune on the radio, set to a soft rock station. Suddenly, he wanted to know all about her, find whatever it was in her that could lift those iron weights in his soul. Find out how she could fill a room with light.

"What's it like, being a plant geneticist? What do you do? How does a plant geneticist fill her day?"

She turned to him in surprise, soft hair shifting on her shoulders. A fleeting expression crossed her face, one he was unable to decipher, the merest hint of darkness, as if a bird's wing had come between her and the sun. Then it was gone.

But when she answered, her voice was light and amused, and he wondered if he'd imagined the darkness. It was almost impossible to connect this woman with any kind of darkness.

The full, luscious mouth turned up at the corners. "It's sort of hard to explain, and boringly technical."

"I went to school," he said softly. Actually he had two master's degrees. One in military history and one in political science. From the days in which he tried really hard to understand the world. Those days were gone. Now he just tried to defend his little corner of it and survive. "I could try to follow."

She stirred something with a wooden spoon, tapped it against the pot, and put the spoon on a ceramic dish. Man, whatever it was she was cooking, it smelled heavenly.

She switched the burner off. "Okay, it's done, but it will take about ten minutes to settle. Why don't we sit at the table and enjoy our wine?"

"Sounds good."

She'd set two places, at right angles instead of across from each other. They were so close he could smell that flowery something above whatever was cooking on the stove. So close he could touch her without any effort at all. He picked up his glass and took another big gulp.

Goddamn it. Even the fucking wine was perfect.

She sipped her wine, head tilted to one side as she studied him.

"Coming back to what we were talking about, I'm really sorry if I gave the wrong impression. I didn't mean you *can't* understand what I do, in the sense of being unable to. What I meant is that, like most jobs, what I do day to day is the tip of the iceberg, and you'd have to know what I did yesterday and what I plan to do tomorrow to get the full picture. The short version is I research how Mother Nature designed plant life, and then think of ways to improve on that. The big picture is really exciting because in a way we're unlocking the secrets to life itself. But the day-to-day stuff is really tedious and boring. In the research lab we spend all our time peering into microscopes, checking cultures in petri dishes, and meticulously recording minute changes—punctuated by days in the field, checking crop rows, measuring growth by millimeters. Not exciting in any way unless you're a botany nerd. I imagine your job is hard to describe too. If you could tell me without having to kill me afterwards."

She smiled and Max tensed.

Here it was. The SEAL thing.

Women just couldn't get past it. Some women treated SEALs like action figures with guns, men able to leap tall buildings in a single bound. The thing was, SEALs weren't supermen. They weren't a special breed of man with superhuman abilities. They were just determined, relentless men who developed specialized skills by working like fiends. What they could do they learned to do the hard way. They worked hard, fought hard, often bled and died.

They were warriors, but they also learned languages and orienteering and history, and had to know how to dig a well, apply a splint, and engineer a road.

Most people couldn't get past the fighting thing.

He couldn't count the women who'd watched his face avidly as they asked him how many men he'd killed. Sometimes they looked at him in disgust as they asked it, as if he were some hired gun. A barely domesticated animal.

Sometimes the avid curiosity morphed into a desire that had a sick taste to it, and that turned his stomach. Because clearly they liked the idea of fucking a killer.

Either way, there could be no explaining what he did.

"I wouldn't kill you," he said softly. "No matter what you've been told. It's a myth."

Oh man. He couldn't kill her, he couldn't hurt her in any way. Seeing Paige sitting next to him, with that soft, lightly-tanned, smooth skin, pretty face open and smiling, friendly and kind . . . she was everything he'd ever fought for. The idea of hurting a woman or a child had always made him physically sick. Paige, hurt . . . *God.*

Paige looked him straight in the eyes, watched him openly. He had no idea what she was seeing, but she suddenly nodded her head, as if confirming something. "No," she said. "You wouldn't hurt me."

"Damn straight," he answered.

There was an electric moment of silence. Max let out his breath in a slow exhale. There was a lot of meaning behind her words. At one level, of course he wasn't going to hurt her, kill her. But the deeper meaning was she felt he wasn't a man to be feared.

Max could hardly remember not being big and strong. By the time he was twelve, he'd shot to six feet and looked sixteen. No one messed with him, and if they did, they were sorry.

The life he lived, particularly after joining the navy and passing BUD/S, had made him even bigger and stronger and meaner-looking. He *was* mean. Fuck with him and you'd regret it. But he chose his battles. He was not out of control and he resented it when a woman treated him like someone in an action movie or a violence addict.

"So," Paige said softly. "Why don't we not talk about our work and talk about something else? Like Max here."

At her feet, Max's tail thumped. There was something about the way the dog was sitting next to her, totally focussed . . .

Max shifted the tablecloth, and—yup. The dog had his head on Paige's thigh. Something he could identify with. He'd like to have his head on Paige's thigh, too.

He frowned at Paige. "Are you feeding him under the table?"

She winced. "Busted."

"That's not good," he said primly, taking the moral high ground, trying hard to keep a straight face as he watched her reaction.

Her skin was fascinating, it signalled every emotion. Right now she was slightly flushed with embarrassment as if she'd been caught with her hand in the cookie jar.

"I know," she said earnestly. "Don't think I don't know it's wrong, I do. After I got Max at the pound, I read up. I'm a researcher, I know how to gain expertise. I read thousands of pages on dog care, and everyone stressed that dogs shouldn't eat from the table. It's bad for them and fosters bad habits." She thunked her forehead with the palm of her hand. "I *know* this. But—just look at him. He pulls at your heartstrings. How can I resist?"

Max leaned over. Doggy Max swivelled his muzzle to him, suddenly alert to the fact that maybe another chump was at the table. Someone else to scam.

His tail thumped more slowly now, as if his energy had been suddenly depleted. He whined and shivered, looking pathetic, whipped. He inched closer to Max, but cautiously, as if Max might have a hidden stick with which to beat him, and wasn't the man he'd spent the entire day with, playing on the beach.

As Max watched, the dog slowly, tremblingly lowered himself to the floor, laying his muzzle on his front paws, as if too weak to hold up his head.

Max raised his head. Paige met his gaze then rolled her eyes.

"Don't tell me, I know." She sighed. "You'd think he just came out of some concentration camp where they whipped and starved him. Instead of having just been fed."

"You fall for it, though," he accused. "Hook, line and sinker."

"Over and over again," she agreed. "What can I say? I'm a total wuss."

They met each other's eyes again and burst out laughing.

It surprised Max. The laugh came straight up from his belly. Genuine, carefree, unstoppable. The first time he'd laughed, really laughed, in . . . in years.

And hard on the heels of that laughter, something else, something sharp and alive, moving fast, like a shark in the water. Dangerous. Subterranean. Irresistible.

Sexual desire, of a nature and intensity he'd never felt before, whooshing in like a tsunami onto a dry beach.

He watched her at the table—so pretty and alive, so whole, so easy to be with—with her golden-brown hair and eyes the color of the Pacific a few steps outside the door. Her light golden shoulders gleamed. They were covered by the thin straps of her dress with no signs of a bra. Was she wearing one? He didn't dare lower his gaze but he had excellent peripheral vision. He didn't think so.

Oh God.

Just a thin layer of cotton covering those breasts. Perfect, round breasts. His palms itched with the desire to touch them, run his fingers over that smooth, smooth skin.

Everything itched. Desire skittered under his skin like fire, so intense it was almost painful. It was as if he'd never had sex before, every molecule of his body turning around and aligning itself to hers, like iron filings to a magnet.

"Don't tell anyone at work that I have no backbone when it comes to my dog," Paige said, pouring some more wine into his glass. "I have a reputation as a hard-ass."

She looked up at him and froze, her eyes widening, that pretty mouth rounding into an "O" at the expression on his face. It was the exact moment he imagined that mouth around his cock. He gritted his teeth against a groan at the image in his head.

Paige was no dummy and she was a woman. They seemed to have a whole slew of extrasensory perceptions that went into alleyways where men couldn't follow and which allowed them to read men's minds.

His mind wasn't hard to read. What he wanted, fiercely, was right there on his face. He wanted *her.*

He was as hard as a rock, so hard it felt as if his dick were a separate thing, not part of his body. A stone cylinder glued to his belly, heavy and intractable.

He didn't plan what happened next—it just surged up out of the moment, unstoppable, irresistible.

Reaching out, he covered her hand with his. Her skin was as soft as it looked, the hand warm and delicate. At the touch of her hand, he became even harder, more blood racing to his cock. It felt like his entire body simply went off-line as his dick came online.

Everything he'd felt this past year—pain, anger, despair—vanished in a wash of incandescent heat blazing throughout his body, from his toes to the top of his head. Blasting away everything except pure, red-hot desire for this one woman.

He looked at his hand over hers and felt more heat wash over him. His hand was larger, darker, stronger, angled over hers. A mental image of the two of them exploded in his head. This is exactly what they'd look like in bed. His larger, darker, stronger body over hers, moving deeply in hers . . .

He closed his eyes at the image and breathed the intensity out.

He opened them again to find her watching him, looking slightly anxious. But she was also deep pink with some strong emotion he hoped to God was at least one millionth of the lust he felt, her mouth open as if she couldn't pull in enough air.

God knows he couldn't. There was no air in his lungs, just a burning sensation. Heat suffused him, inside and out.

They stared at each other. She had the most amazing eyes, a light blue with green streaks, shimmering as if the ocean were at her feet and reflected in her eyes.

He breathed in a gasp. Said words that were wrenched straight from his chest without any prior thought at all. "I want you."

Oh, fuck. The words were out there, stark and simple, and he couldn't call them back. He barely recognized his own voice—low and guttural, as if the words came from somewhere deep inside him. And they had. They came from his very core.

He'd played the sex game all his life. He liked women and he liked sex, and though he wasn't as slick as some, he knew how to say enough sweet honeyed words to get a woman into his bed. Some wanted romantic words, some wanted sexy talk. Some didn't require much talking at all.

He'd never just come out with it like that. Crude and simple. *I want you.*

He scrabbled for more words, better words, but they just weren't coming. In his head was heat and the image of them tangled together, skin to skin, so close they could feel each other's heartbeat. He had a sensory hallucination for a second where he could *feel* what it would be like entering her, parting her lower lips with his cock . . .

He tightened all the muscles in his stomach and groin because he was a second away from coming.

He opened his mouth and all that came out was air.

Since there weren't any more words he could say, he simply sat there, trying to control his breathing. Trying to give the impression of a man who was in control, who *had* control, when it was slipping through his fingers.

There'd been a flicker of something in her eyes. God, what?

Her small hand flexed under his. For a terrible moment, he thought she was going to refuse. Slide her hand out from under his and say no.

At the thought, it was if his chest filled with barbed wire. He was a strategic thinker—in the battlefield, under fire, he could always see the next step and the one after that.

Right now? He had no sense of what he'd do if she said no. None. He wanted her so much, it felt unthinkable that they weren't going straight to bed to start having sex just as quickly as their legs could carry them.

Shit, if she said no, he couldn't even drop to his knees and beg her. His fucking leg would crumple. He'd fall over flat on his ass.

But the god of wounded warriors smiled on him, after a whole year of fucking with him.

"I know," she said softly. "I can see that you want me."

He froze. She could see it? How? He felt as big as a house, but she couldn't see him below the waist. Obviously his face showed his ballooning need. He hoped whatever she saw didn't scare her.

He took in another breath in a gasp. Tried to get all the words out before speech was beyond him, because they needed to be said.

"I don't know what you'll decide, but if I do get lucky, then I need to give full disclosure. I haven't had sex in two years. I was deployed in—well, a bad, sandy place for a year, and I spent the year after that in hospitals and rehab clinics trying to put myself together. I don't have any condoms with me at all. Coming here it never even occurred to me because until about two minutes ago, sex wasn't part of my life anymore. And now I can't think of anything else but sex with you. But this no-condom thing has to be taken into account. I do know I don't have any diseases. None. Bloodsuckers at the hospital drained me of half my blood, taking tests, and I'm clean."

"Oh!" She gave a faint smile. "I—ahm. Me, too. I had a checkup just a couple of months ago. I haven't had sex for a year—too busy, really. And . . . the work I do, it sometimes takes me to test fields and research stations in remote parts of the world. Some in countries that are not, ahm, always completely stable. So my company offers its female researchers birth control. We get monthly shots. I've just had mine."

Max scowled, sex wiped instantly from his mind. "Your company sends you to *dangerous places?*" he breathed, the thought driving him slightly insane for a second.

Max had close-up intimate knowledge of what bad places were like. He knew hellholes the way a suburban dad knows the potholes on his street. The idea of smiling, delicate, pretty Paige in some of the places he'd been horrified him.

"What the *hell* are your bosses thinking, sending you—"

She shut him up by placing her mouth over his, swamping him with heat. Her mouth tasted exactly as he thought it would—sweet and hot. Fresh and exciting.

It was a brief kiss, two mouths meeting, but he broke away gasping as if burned. He looked at her narrow-eyed as she watched him, head cocked to one side as if he were a puzzle.

She was the goddamned puzzle. Max knew kisses, he knew sex, he knew women, and he knew his reaction to women. This was all completely new.

Fuck.

He'd nearly come in his pants with a mere kiss. A kiss that lasted two seconds, tops.

It wasn't supposed to be like this. Max was The Man. Cool and in control, in bed and out. Not a man so excited that a touch to the mouth damn near set him off.

Probably it was two years of abstinence. Yeah, that was it. Two long years with only his fist in the Sandbox, and in the hospital nothing at all because his dick was a dead piece of meat between his legs. It had been painful to breathe. Sex just hadn't been on his radar.

Maybe what he'd just felt was some . . . some anomaly in the space-time continuum. A one-off.

Try it again.

His touched his mouth to hers and again felt that electric shock.

She'd closed her eyes. They slowly opened when he lifted his mouth. The pupils were a little dilated and she looked dazed. Good, maybe he wasn't completely alone in this, whatever this was. Because it wasn't sex. Or at least it wasn't sex as he knew it.

Again.

She watched him, watched as he moved his face closer to hers, closing her eyes at the last second. This time the kiss was longer, deeper, nerve endings concentrated in his mouth as he tasted her—one long, slow stroke of the tongue, her mouth silky soft and delicious. She tasted of wine and sunshine and woman.

When he lifted his mouth, she made a soft sound. "Max?"

Under the table, a scrabbling of furry limbs and a soft woof. He snapped his fingers and patted the air. "Not you, boy. Me."

Paige smiled.

"I'm right here," he whispered, reaching out a hand to cup

her neck and bring her back to him. Another kiss, deeper, longer, sweeter, hotter.

When he pulled back she searched his eyes. "Where are we going with this?"

For the first time, he chanced a smile. He no longer felt as if his head were going to explode any second now. The smile felt odd, unused facial muscles working. "To bed," he whispered. "I hope."

Hand still cupped around her neck, he bent forward until their foreheads touched. "I think I remember how it's done. But I have to warn you, I don't have smooth moves and smooth words." They'd been blasted right out of him.

Her lips curled up. "Maybe not smooth words, but those are the right words. I don't like players."

Nail it down. Get it right. For all he knew, in the two years he'd been out of the scene, the rules had changed.

"That's a yes?"

Paige pulled away, angled her head, observed him for a full minute. He let her. If he passed muster, he was just about to become the luckiest guy in the universe.

"Yes."

Yes!

CHAPTER FOUR

This was so unlike her, Paige marvelled at herself. She was really picky and fussy when it came to men. How did she end up saying yes to a man she hadn't even known for twenty-four hours?

Because of all those muscles? Even if he was very lean it was obvious he was a big man. Give him another couple of months and she was sure he'd bulk back up. Muscles were good, though she'd never really thought of herself as a Jersey Shore kind of gal.

She wasn't. She was cerebral. True, his size was a plus, and that macho air—which she usually disliked—surprisingly worked for her. But macho wasn't enough. He was an officer, he was a SEAL. Presumably he had smarts, and so far he seemed bright enough, but they'd barely conversed much beyond generalities.

So—not so much the muscles or the macho or the mind.

Nope.

He'd been kind to her dog.

She'd have berated herself for her stupidity if it weren't for the fact that her entire body was tingling as he brought her hand to his mouth, eyes never leaving hers.

His mouth was warm, but she knew that. When he'd kissed her, the warmth of his mouth had spread all through her. There was a tiny bite of beard around his lips. He'd recently shaved but he looked like he'd had a heavy beard.

He kept her hand in his and rose. She rose with him, and into his arms, the most natural thing in the world. He was very tall. She was so close to him she had to tilt her head back.

He had that grim look again, only maybe it wasn't grimness. Maybe it was just his default expression—the expression of a hard man who'd seen bad things. And though he didn't seem like the type of man to talk about it, she imagined his leg was hurting.

"I'd give anything to pick you up and carry you to the bedroom," he said. A long finger was tracing the contours of her face. Just the merest touch, but it felt exciting and tender at the same time. "It would be romantic and it would get us there faster. A twofer."

She laughed. "Well, I've never been carried anywhere, so I guess I don't know what I'm missing."

"And I don't know where your bedroom is," he pointed out. "So I couldn't carry you there anyway."

One hand was still in his, the other had gone around his back. She didn't have any spare hands so she indicated with her chin toward the back of the house. "Second room to the right. The first is my study."

He kissed the tip of her nose, kept his face close to hers. "Well then, Paige Waring. Why don't you lead us to it?" His wine-scented breath washed over her.

So. She was going to do this. Amazing. She watched his face for another long moment. Not making up her mind, because it wasn't her mind that was involved here. Just checking her body that this was what it wanted.

Oh, yeah.

His face was so interesting. Hard planes, weather-beaten skin that made him look older than he probably was; dark, observant eyes; hard-looking mouth that had been surprisingly soft when kissing her.

And there was . . . something. What? What made this man out of all the men she'd ever met the one man she'd go to bed with after the shortest acquaintance in her social history?

Whatever it was, it was potent, because now that the decision had been made—and her body, having been duly consulted, enthusiastically shouted *Yes!*—she couldn't wait.

"Come with me then, soldier."

He smiled. "That would be sailor, but you bet I'm coming with you."

He limped. If Paige hadn't had her arm around his waist she wouldn't have noticed, but there was a slight hesitation every time he put his weight on his left leg.

Max trotted right behind them, tongue lolling out of his mouth, wondering if this was a new game.

"We're being followed," she whispered.

He glanced down at her. "I noticed. I think the kid needs to stay outside, don't you?"

She nodded. "Wouldn't want him to lose his innocence. He's only eight months old."

"Yeah, too young for this."

They reached her room and he gently closed the door in

Max's muzzle. There was a puzzled bark from the other side of the door. "Sorry, big guy," Max called out. "Wait till you're old enough to have a beer. Now." He put his hands on her hips and looked her up and down. "Oh God," he whispered. "I don't know where to start."

She smiled. "From the top."

The setting sun outside the window shone directly into the room, bathing it with a golden light. Everything in her room seemed to glow, as if enchanted. She had a small collection of silver vases which gleamed on her dresser. There was utter silence, broken only by the silver surf splashing on the beach. A moment out of time, magical.

He seemed to understand the magic of the moment too, holding her eyes as he slowly undid the buttons of her dress until it hung open. It was too hot for a bra so she stood before him in panties and an open dress.

He closed his eyes briefly then opened them, gaze dark and hot. "Did you wear those panties just to drive me crazy?"

She looked down. Pale pink silk and lace. They were pretty and they were expensive, too. She had to wear an anonymous lab coat at work and it always gave her a thrill to know she had on sexy, uber-feminine undergarments. She met his eyes. "There's a matching bra, too. I can put it on if you like. So you can it take back off."

He sighed. "Tempting as that sounds, I'll pass." He placed his big hands on her shoulders, leaving them there for a moment. A cool breeze fluttered her curtains, filling the room with the scent of sunshine and ocean. His hands were warm and heavy, the skin of his palms slightly abrasive as he smoothed them over her shoulders, shucking off the dress.

It was pointless trying to cover herself with her hands, so she stood straight under his scrutiny. That warm, dark gaze felt like hands caressing her as he looked her up and down, finally meeting her eyes again.

"Man," he breathed and she nearly laughed. As a compliment, it was more effective than any flowery phrases had ever been. The heavy hands drifted down her sides, thumbs hooking in her panties. A swipe of his hands and they fell. She stepped out of them and stepped out of her shoes.

Though her heels were low, it felt as if he grew much taller once she was in her bare feet, standing before her fully dressed while she was naked.

"Here, feel how much I want you," he whispered, voice low and hoarse. Shockingly, he took her hand and placed it right over his groin. Instinctively, her hand curled around him, his penis so hot she could feel the heat through the material of his jeans. At her touch, his penis moved beneath her palm as blood raced through it, becoming even harder.

He stood still under her touch, the only sign of his arousal a dark red wash over his cheekbones.

That convinced her more than anything else that she had nothing to fear—his utter stillness. He was watching her carefully, as if to take his cues from her.

"Now you undress me." That deep voice grew even lower.

"Okay." Paige stepped closer, so close her naked breasts brushed against his shirt front. She reached up and undid the top button of his white shirt.

To her surprise, her hands were trembling, with excitement, with trepidation. This was so unlike her other sexual experiences, where things happened fast. There was a solemn, deliberate pace he'd established, each step toward the lovemaking like a little ceremony. Definitely foreplay, though he wasn't even touching her, just watching her.

And yet it was almost unbearably exciting. She was so aware of everything—of the gathering shadows in her room, of the silence, of the sound and feel of her breathing. Her skin tingled with anticipation as she slowly unbuttoned his shirt. He watched her intently, face expressionless. If she hadn't noticed the high color of arousal in his face, if she couldn't feel the thick column of his penis against her stomach she could almost think he was unaffected by her movements.

Almost.

Her fingers were at the last button before his belt and she stopped, hands hovering over the buckle. She looked up at him and he nodded.

Taking a deep breath, she unbuckled the belt, unzipped his jeans, the back of her fingers brushing against him, hot and hard. His hips jerked and she looked up at him, startled. "Get me out of these clothes fast, please."

O-kay.

She was feeling a sense of urgency herself, like swimming in a river that was picking up speed, rushing toward rapids. She had to stand on tiptoe for a second to push the shirt off his shoulders. Half a minute later, she knelt to pull off his jeans and briefs and take off his sneakers.

When she rose, he was naked. The most powerful man she'd ever laid eyes upon. His body was utterly unlike any other naked male body she'd ever seen. Almost as if he were a male of a different species. His body was a reflection of the life he'd led. Broad, hard muscles defined by battle and not a gym.

He was thinner than his body type would indicate, no doubt because of the injuries. Each muscle was hard and tightly defined, like an anatomy drawing in living flesh.

And the scars. Oh, God, the scars. She'd seen them on the beach but out of politeness had kept her eyes trained on his. Now she could look all she liked.

She sucked in her breath, fingers reaching out. The leg was bad enough, but this . . . . The scars were everywhere, some thin and white, some with thick raised keloid tissue. She touched them delicately, each scar representing untold pain. She traced a thick scar over his left side, right under the brown nipple. Obviously his rib cage had stopped what should have been a killing blow. There were two round, puckered scars even she could recognize as bullet wounds low on his hip. Together with the one on his shoulder it made a little trifecta of pain.

He was alive by a miracle.

He stilled her hand, flattening his over hers. Under her palm, she could feel hard muscle, prickly chest hair, the strong beat of his heart.

Their eyes met. "I'm so sorry," she whispered.

"It's over," he said. "Right now, all I want to think about is this." He smoothed a big hand over her hip, across her belly, laying his palm lightly on her mound. "Open for me, Paige," he whispered.

There was no question. Her feet shifted, his hand slid between her legs, cupped her. She huffed out a little breath of excitement. It was as if a sun bloomed there, between her thighs. His fingers stroked her, her flesh so sensitive there she broke out in goose bumps.

One finger circled, slid inside, and her knees weakened.

She clenched around his finger and the color deepened over his cheekbones. He bent down and kissed her, not touching her anywhere but with his mouth and his hand between her legs and oh, when his tongue touched hers, she clenched tightly again around his finger. He sucked in a breath when he felt it, the breath coming from her lungs.

Another slow swirl of his tongue in her mouth. "We need to take this to the bed before I fall down," he said against her lips.

She smiled, mouth so close to his she felt his breath. She was vibrating with heat, with excitement, and couldn't formulate words. "Hmm."

Max turned, stretched out on the bed, held out a big hand. "You're going to have to be on top. Sorry. This is going to be a huge incentive to me to gain more flexibility in my leg. I like the missionary position."

"I'll just bet you do," she said with a half-smile. Oh yeah, this was a man who'd like to be in command.

Paige looked down at him, at this huge, dark man on her pristine white bedspread, taking up half the bed. Almost every muscle he had was tense, in relief. One muscle, in particular. Was it a muscle? She knew her botany but not her anatomy.

Whatever it was, it was huge and hard as steel and utterly fascinating. His penis was dark with blood, the thick tip even darker, and almost reached his navel. She could see his heartbeat in the tip, trembling slightly with each beat of his heart. Though she would have sworn it was impossible, it thickened even more under her gaze.

She was supposed to put that inside her?

But then her vagina pulsed once, sharply. Her body was

readying itself for him, all by itself. Her body wanted this, no question.

How strange. With her previous lovers, she realized, she had to almost coax herself into arousal—but not now. It was as if some outside force were taking her over, or maybe a really primitive part of her, one she'd never been aware of, was coming to the fore.

He curled his fingers up. "Come to me, Paige." That low, deep, utterly male voice was irresistible. Feeling carried by forces beyond her control, she placed one knee on the bed and swung herself over him.

If you'd asked her, she'd have said she preferred the missionary position, too, at least at first. If you'd asked her, she'd have said it was awkward being on top right away, she'd feel clumsy clambering over him, wouldn't know where to put her knees and elbows.

But nobody asked, and she found herself flowing on top of him like water, the only thought in her overheated head to try to touch as much of him with as much of her as possible. In a moment, she was stretched out on top of him, his arms holding her tightly, kissing her savagely, as if they were long-lost lovers reunited after years of separation.

One hand was holding her to him, the other reached down to open her up. Oh God, she gasped when he touched her again, she was even more sensitive there than before. Every nerve ending in her body congregating right . . . *there*.

She moaned and he stiffened under her, kissing her more deeply, holding her more tightly. She was opened up over him and he started sliding along her lips without penetrating, so slowly she could feel in turn that broad head, the steely shaft, his thick pubic hair against her. Then back, slowly. Forward. Back. The motions speeding up. With each passage, she grew hotter and wetter. He was moving faster now, passing over her clitoris with a little explosion of feeling each time.

Explosions of feelings everywhere. Her mouth, her hands, clinging to his hard shoulders as if she'd fall off a cliff if she didn't hang on tight, the insides of her thighs lightly abraded by the hairs on his legs, the hard muscles of his stomach brushing against hers with every movement.

Faster. Harder. Hotter.

She was on top, but not in control. He was doing everything—kissing her so hard she was breathing through his mouth, his hips moving so fast the bed started creaking, the friction burning her up.

He must have felt something: her muscles going slack as she began that luscious slide into orgasm, her breath caught in her lungs, that inward turning . . . something. Because the moment she started clenching around his penis, he lifted her slightly, thrust his hips up, and, oh God! entered her.

He was already moving, hard and fast, somehow timing his thrusts to her orgasm as they rocked together in some primordial rhythm that sucked her under, as if the climax were some warm tidal sea where she lost her sense of self completely, connected to life by her mouth to his and him rocking inside her.

Floating, rocking, detached from earth. Slippery and hot, clenching around him—not only with her vagina but with her arms and legs—until they were one creature, one being, fused together.

The pulses were starting to die down when he made a noise in her mouth, his movements inside her becoming short and hard—so fast she thought the friction would burn her up—and he started coming. He swelled inside her, impossibly, and came in huge hot jets and that set her off again, this time in tight clenches so hard she could feel it in her stomach muscles.

They slowed, quieted, and all the tension of the orgasm left her body in one huge whoosh, leaving her sprawled all over this huge man.

They were sticky with sweat and their juices, a feeling she'd ordinarily hate. With any other man, she'd have gotten out of bed as fast as possible to head into the shower.

Not now. Because, though they were sweaty and sticky, there was an amazing feeling of closeness, as if she'd become part of his body or he part of hers. It had never occurred to her before how incredibly *intimate* sex was.

It wasn't just a pleasant pastime. It was a melding of bodies.

She felt every part of his body. His heart thumping against her breasts, the beats hard and steady. The crinkly chest and body hair like a little mattress, or like lying on a lawn. She smiled at that thought and opened her mouth to tell him when she felt him draw a huge breath, lifting her up.

"That was fun," his deep voice rumbled. "Let's do it again."

Paige laughed, her stomach muscles brushing his.

He was serious, still hard inside her.

He gave one experimental thrust, as if asking permission, moving easily now that they'd both come.

Did she want another round right now? Hmmm. She felt really relaxed. Sex with him was exciting but really . . . intense.

Another smooth stroke, a kiss dropped on her shoulder.

Another. Oh God, he was heating her up.

She opened her mouth to say *okay* when her stomach suddenly rumbled.

"Well, I guess I have my answer," he said good-naturedly.

And then his stomach rumbled.

He tilted her chin up with a long finger and waited until she opened her eyes. He smiled. "I vote we go eat ourselves silly then come back to bed. What do you say?"

And Paige Waring, staid scientist, said, "Sounds like a plan."

Oh man, he was in heaven. Max sat up and leaned back against something really soft. Silk, maybe. Or satin? The headboard was really comfortable and looked like something a Pascha would have. The bed, too. Real girly stuff. Amazingly frilly sheets with a sort of flounce around the bottom.

He sniffed appreciatively. Everything smelled so nice, too. Even over the smell of sex, which made him horny.

Everything made him horny now. It was as if his dick had had an "off" switch that had now been switched back on. Permanently.

Paige was taking a quick shower. She'd seen the interest on his face when she said that and shook a finger at him so he stayed in bed like a good boy.

There was plenty of time.

He hoped.

Paige came out—the bathroom door opening, flowery-smelling steam billowing out—wearing a thin silk robe, wet hair hanging down her back. Shower Paige. To be added to

Beach Paige, and Scientist Paige, and Dinner Date Paige and Naked Paige.

He liked the last one best.

She smiled at him as he swung his legs over the side of the bed. "I don't have anything that could possibly fit you, so I guess you should put these on." And tossed him his briefs.

He caught them one-handed, and swallowed. Put them on, followed her to the living room. Max the dog was leaping in delight at seeing them again after all of an hour's absence. "So . . . no clothes of absent boyfriends around?"

Not very subtle, but he suddenly had a burning need to know.

"Nope." She gave him a sunny smile. "Nary a one."

"So . . . this thing we're having . . ."

"This *thing?*" A little frown appeared between her ash-brown eyebrows."

Max felt like choking. "Yeah, this thing. This affair." Words were sticking in his throat like razor blades, each one sharp. "Whatever it is we're having, it's exclusive, right?"

Her head cocked and she just stared at him. A little sweat trickled down his bare back.

"Just you and me," he clarified. "Exclusive."

"Just you and me," she repeated, and nodded. "Yes."

He let out his breath. "So . . . we're a thing?"

Paige closed her eyes. "You're missing a good chunk of vocabulary."

"Yeah." He knew. He could barely think, let alone speak. The only thing he knew was that Paige was his, was a part of his life now. He'd seen a glimpse of the sun and he wasn't going to let it go.

"Okay." She opened her eyes and looked at him. "I will forgive your total inability to express yourself adequately and state that we are now 'going out.' Do you want me to say we're 'going steady'?"

Tension left his body. "Will you go to the prom with me?"

She laughed and took one step forward. He took a step forward. They met and he kissed her. And kissed her. He didn't consider himself a master kisser, but this felt like something else, like a big fat dividing line. Before and After.

Before was darkness and solitude. After was warmth and light.

Max jumped them. After was also the dog, wriggling with happiness at their feet.

Paige broke away, breathing hard. Her lips were red, swollen, glistening, just as her little cunt had been. The thought nearly unmanned him.

They had a "thing" now. She'd said so. She wasn't going anywhere, and neither was he. So why the urgency? Why this prickling feeling that everything would dissipate like smoke unless he grabbed her now?

She stepped back, watching his eyes. Maybe understanding his compulsion? With a flutter of silk she disappeared into the kitchen, coming back out with a tray. The dog was leaping and dancing at her feet, giving small yips of joy at the smell of food.

"I think at this point we need to put him outside— otherwise we'll never hear the end of it."

"Oh yeah," she sighed.

She snapped her fingers and Max wriggled happily. When she opened the door and pointed outside, he collapsed on the threshold, legs splayed, whining as if shown the door to hell itself. Paige snapped her fingers again. He rose trembling to his feet and slinked outside. Amazed that she would do this terrible thing to him. She closed the door in his reproachful face.

Max started barking immediately, loud barks guaranteed to wake any neighbors within a mile. They looked at each other, listening to Max. When they heard the sound of his claws tearing at the wooden door, Paige stepped close.

"Max! Bad dog! No barking!"

She might as well have been talking to the wind. The intensity of the barks increased.

This was ridiculous. He slapped the door. "Max! Stop!"

The noise stopped immediately. There was a faint whine and a yip and then nothing.

"Does one have to go to officer school to be able to do that?" she asked, tilting her head up to him.

Max smiled down at her. "It helps."

"I don't want to be commanded." There was a little pucker of worry between her eyebrows and he smoothed it away.

"I don't want to command you." Oh man, no. "Why would I want to do that?"

She shrugged, the light silk sliding off one shoulder. No, he didn't want to command her, but he did want to do something else.

It filled his head until he could think of nothing else. Max was forgotten, food was forgotten, the only thing filling his head was Paige, naked underneath a thin silk robe. It wouldn't have made any difference if she'd been wearing chain mail.

She looked down at him, blushed, then looked up. "I thought you were hungry?"

"Mm." Heat filled his head, his hands itched. The only thing that could make them stop itching was touching her. It took only a second to untie the robe and slip it off her shoulders and then she was in his arms, naked, soft breasts against his chest.

She'd seen precisely what his body wanted. It was visible to all, sticking out from his groin. Men really had nowhere to hide.

But—but she was affected, too. The signs were less visible, but there, if you knew where to look. Dilated pupils, a slight sheen on her face, her left breast trembling with the beat of her heart.

And there, that sweet spot between her legs. He ran his hand down her back, between her buttocks, lower and . . . yes. Oh yeah. Soft and hot and wet. The female equivalent of a hard-on.

Suddenly, his leg wouldn't hold him anymore, and not just his leg. His entire spine had melted, gone liquid, flowed into his cock, and then solidified.

Kissing her, he reached out with his foot, hooked a chair, dropped his briefs, sat down, and pulled her down on top of him. Just opened her up, pulled his cock away from his stomach and shoved it into her because if he didn't, he'd die.

They sat like that, a little sexy tableau, Woman on Man. Paige's arms were around his back, face buried in his neck, his cock buried to the hilt in her.

"Whoa," he said and stopped, because what could he say? He hadn't planned this at all. He thought they'd eat together and maybe he could coax her into another round in bed eventually. Or maybe tomorrow morning if she fell asleep immediately. This—this was unplanned and completely unstoppable. His body had reacted faster than his head.

He looked down past her shoulder. Bright shiny hair, pale golden skin, strong sleek back, the indent of a small waist, buttocks sitting on his thighs.

It was, hands down, the most erotic sight he'd ever seen.

"Are, um, we okay here?" Because maybe she'd actually wanted to eat instead of being jumped.

In answer, she lowered her mouth to his shoulder, took a little nip, then kissed him.

His cock leaped inside her at the tiny bite. He lifted his hips while holding hers and slid in and out, once, testing.

She remained lax against him, eyes closed, a faint smile on her face. She sighed.

Okay.

Oh, yeah.

Another slide in, pulling out. And again. She lifted her face slightly and took his earlobe in her mouth, and took another little bite.

He lost it.

Holding her tightly, he slammed into her, establishing a hard rhythm, trying and failing to hold back. He couldn't. It was as if his life depended on getting as deeply into her as he could and staying there as long as he could.

Thank God she was with him, growing wetter by the minute—otherwise they'd catch on fire.

Harder, faster . . . they were rocking in the chair now and a dim part of his brain hoped they wouldn't topple over, because there was no way he could stop.

Paige moved her head again and kissed him, her mouth as soft as her cunt, and it set him off. Rocket man.

He held her hard against him while a hot wire sparked down his back and exploded through his cock, and he came in hot, fierce spurts that went on forever.

Just as his spasms were dying down, she exhaled sharply in his ear—raising goose bumps all over his body—and clenched tightly around him, as if her cunt were trying to hold on to him.

Oh man, he wasn't going anywhere—he was staying right here, feeling her entire body shaking with her climax.

When it was over, he was holding her tightly, panting. Maybe holding her too tightly. Was he hurting her? He slowly relaxed his grip, shifting to make her more comfortable.

They were wet where they were joined and every move made a small noise. He rubbed a hand over her satiny back, exhausted, as content as he'd ever been in his life.

"Uh oh." Paige wriggled on him a little. He swelled inside her, as if he hadn't just had the most explosive orgasm in his life. "Are we ever going to eat? Or are we just going to sit here until they find our dead bodies?"

It was a thought. At some point in June his XO would arrive. Wouldn't find him, would check with Paige, and there they'd be. Two corpses, still together, covered in cobwebs.

He sighed. "We'll eat. Sometime next week. Maybe."

CHAPTER FIVE

April 5

My gosh, good sex is better than Prozac as a mood lifter, Paige thought five days later as she walked back to her apartment after taking Maximilian for an afternoon walk. He was unusually frisky, leaping and barking and making her laugh. The kids on the beach made her laugh. The cool little wavelets frothing over her feet made her laugh.

It was Friday, Maxwell was on his way home from a doctor's appointment, and they'd spend the evening and the night together as they had every evening and every night for the past four days. And the weekend—she shivered. Two full days with him. Forty-eight hours. Non-stop.

Oh yeah. Sex with Max was better than any mood-lifting drug known to mankind.

Even the dark cloud of worry about Silvia was manageable. She hadn't heard from Silvia since last Monday, B.M. Before Max. When she still had the capacity to fret and worry. It seemed to have left her body, together with all her sexual inhibitions. And all that empty space? Filled by her new lover.

Maybe Silvia had pulled a Paige? Maybe she'd found herself a super lover and had disappeared for a week somewhere?

After all, she was in Argentina, a country full of Latin lovers. Of course, there was no Latin lover on earth who could compete with Max, but still. Paige imagined having a laughing girl-fest with Silvia over a glass of wine at that swanky place on De Mott Street. *I was worried about you*, she'd say, and Silvia would smirk, her dark eyes dancing with amusement.

"OK. Got it. Not to worry," Paige said out loud to the imaginary Silvia, bending to ruffle the fur behind her dog's ears. "I should take a leaf from your book, big boy, and be a little less anxious. Though I'd try not to have that goofy expression on my face."

He was panting and yipping, tongue lolling out of his mouth, in dog heaven. A long walk with his mistress and at the end of it food. What else was needed to be happy?

"Indeed," Paige said, not even annoyed with herself that she was talking out loud to her dog. "What else is needed? Besides fantabulous sex?"

Max yipped in agreement, and she laughed as she opened the door and almost tripped over Max, who was scrambling to get inside, barking wildly because it was food time. Thank God the only neighbor was Max, who had a real soft spot for her Max.

Though, come to think of it, it appeared that human Max was also *her* Max. Now wasn't that delicious?

She shook her head as she reached under the sink, doggy Max's enthusiasm reaching frantic proportions. They'd definitely started *something*, but it was too early to say just what. It was enough that, so far, whatever it was, it was pretty wonderful.

Max was bouncing off the walls. Though doggy Max was like a marine when human Max was around, obeying instantly, he reverted to the slacker teenager he really was in the presence of his mistress.

Paige had one obedience trick in her arsenal. "Only *good dogs* get food." She usually said that in tones that would have been used by an old-time school marm. Sometimes it actually worked, depending on how hungry Max was.

The jumping stopped but the barking didn't, so she sighed and filled his food and water bowls.

Max had said he wouldn't be back before six, which gave her time to get some work done in her study, have a really nice, long, leisurely bath, and start cooking. Heat washed over her as she wondered whether they'd end up eating the food at midnight, as they often did.

After amazing sex.

Oh, God. She sat down abruptly, her legs giving out.

For a moment there, she'd had a sensory memory of being held tightly by him as he moved in her, hovering in a blaze of heat on the knife's edge of an orgasm . . .

She gave a shiver and simply sat for a moment, because her legs wouldn't hold her, flushed red with the memory of this past week.

Max watched her, head cocked, probably wondering what his insane mistress was up to.

Reliving the most intense sexual experiences of her life, that's what. But she couldn't tell him that. He was only eight months old.

Get a grip on yourself. It was so hard to reconcile what she knew of herself with the messages her body was sending her.

Paige was cool and cerebral. A little detached. Always had been. She'd never been ruled by her hormones like her roommate in college had been. Moira had had a real good time in college. Real good. But she'd dropped out because Study of Gross Male Anatomy hadn't been on the curriculum and nothing else had interested her half as much.

Paige had been a straight-A student all the way.

She'd always liked sex, it was one of life's greatest pleasures. Somewhere above *Spaghetti all'Amatriciana* but definitely below that amazing massage she'd had at the Broken Tree Spa overlooking the Pacific. And it had always been a pleasure she could do without when there was no one suitable around.

So that was her experience of sex, which was worlds away from this compulsion, like a dark creature living inside her that filled her head with heated images. Every time she moved, she was reminded of Max, particularly when she sat down.

She, who was so very self-sufficient, couldn't wait for Max to get back from San Francisco.

Not just for the sex, either. She wanted to hear what the doctor said about his leg. She wanted to tell him what an incredible dickhead the project leader was being. Maybe she'd share her worries about Silvia. If he laughed them away, she'd feel better about it. If he took her worries seriously, she might think of contacting someone.

She trusted his judgement absolutely.

That was something new, too. Paige never trusted anyone's judgement as much as she trusted her own. But the few times Max disagreed with her opinion, he made her think. For such a macho man, he had the capacity to reason things out in a way that made sense to her.

She missed him. She wanted him home right now.

It was as if she had this tropism, like a plant to the sun.

She wanted him home, *now*.

Her vagina clenched.

Whoa. She definitely needed to think of something else. Some work ought to do it. There was some data she needed to enter into a spreadsheet and some reports she had to catch up on. Work cooled her down, centered her.

She dove in and was lost to the world when her cell phone rang.

"Hello?"

"Paige!"

She sat up, electrified. "Silvia! Where are you? I've been trying to—"

"Paige, I have to be quick! I've sent you info on Twitter. To Barbie, go check it now. Make sure you put it somewhere safe. Something terrible is happening, Paige. I think we're going to have to go to the FDA. Maybe the FBI."

Paige's eyes widened as she clutched her cell phone. "Where have you—"

"No time, Paige! I've been running away from them all week. I think I've finally found a place where I can be safe. A friend is going to help me cross over into—" The connection was broken and Paige stared at the cell phone's display. She checked the call register. It wasn't Silvia's cell phone number, which was memorized in her SIM card. Silvia was either using someone else's cell or had bought a disposable one.

Something terrible is happening.

The urgency in Silvia's voice spurred her. She accessed Twitter and scrolled. She and Silvia had set up a private communication system—@Barbie1 and @Barbie2—to complain about their bosses. Two years ago, Paige had had what they called a "seagull boss"—he flew in, he crapped all over everything, and then flew out—who was angry at the failed results coming from his pet project. In one notable incident, he threw the hard copy of the failed test—all two hundred pages—in the air, accusing her of not doing her job. Of being a Barbie doll hired for her looks.

Instead of being kicked in the ass, he'd been kicked upstairs, but not before writing an epically negative report on her.

Silvia had been there, and ever since then, they kept a close eye on all the assholes. Currently the biggest asshole in sight was the man overseeing the Argentina project out of Buenos Aires.

Paige looked at the message Silvia had left for her @Barbie1. It was nonsense with a tinyurl in it. Clicking it brought her to a site dedicated to the restoration of Assyrian artifacts, and then to a specific section of the site. Smart girl.

She isolated the section, which was huge—at least six hundred pages, over six hundred kilobytes. But the kicker was in the first ten pages. Paige skimmed the intro to the section, her heart starting to thump in panic.

The test fields of HGHM-1 in Argentina had been planted five years ago, the minimum time the FDA required before applying for permission for human consumption of a new variety. Test results on animals had shown no anomalies. Human testing had not yet begun. But Silvia had gathered data from hospitals and clinics in the surrounding area. The data was preliminary, not all of it collation-ready, but serious enough to warrant an immediate halt to the test trials.

Cancer rates in a radius of two hundred miles had increased by 400 percent over the past five years. Argentinian newspapers were calling it "The Cancer Epidemic." Silvia was the first to connect it to the test fields, which had been kept confidential. Even on a hasty reading, Paige could see that there was a strong case to be made for the fact that her company's new plant variety was massively carcinogenic.

The project had to be terminated immediately, the plants uprooted and destroyed. A whole department of the company would have to shut down, a $30 million dollar investment wiped off the books, the legal department advised that probably a multi-million dollar lawsuit was in the offing. Heads would roll.

Silvia had also sent her a personal message.

On Monday, a car tried to drive me off the road. It was that twisty, winding road I sometimes take to get to Santa Maria. The car tried to run me off the road twice, but there were other cars on the road and it drove off. I was shaken. When I got home, my door was open. They'd trashed my apartment. They took my computer. I took one look and ran. I've kept my cell off so they couldn't track me, and turned it on only to try to call you, but they must have some kind of homing device, because a few seconds into the call, I get static. By "they" I think it's a little rogue operation inside the company's security division. I don't dare use any friends' cell phones. These guys mean business.

I'm in BA right now, staying with friends for a night or two, then moving on. I'm sending this to you from an internet café.

I need to get home somehow. Can you help? I don't think security at headquarters is involved, but you never know, so don't contact them. Right now, I'm thinking FBI.

I'll be checking for a message from you a couple of times a day. Remember it's GMT +3.

God, Paige. Help me. I need to come home. I need to put this into someone's hands.

Her own hands were trembling. Her mind was racing as she eliminated the restoration of Assyrian artifacts section and downloaded only Silvia's file onto her hard drive and then onto her thumb drive. She watched the bar filling while trying to figure out who could be after Silvia.

The most obvious choice for bad guy was the overall project's team leader, Jonathan Finder. He had the psychological profile for it, too. Ambitious and greedy. This was his project and he was making his name with it. It was going to have to be scrapped and would probably cost the company huge amounts of money in reparations. It was the kind of blow that could destroy a career.

Paige had always considered him a lightweight, but even wusses could be driven to violence by fear and greed.

Paige didn't even know where Finder was. He wasn't at her lab, but that didn't mean anything. GenPlant Laboratories ran facilities all over. Four research centers in the continental United States, including the high-security facility on Santo Domingo, and three outside the country. One in India, one in Thailand, and one in Argentina. Finder could be in any of these.

Was he capable of running a rogue cover-up operation?

If she only had something she could take to someone. Even an incriminating email, *something*. If she could go to the section head, Larry Pelton, with something other than wild conjecture, maybe she could stop Finder. Larry definitely had the authority to block Finder, especially if Finder were using GL resources to hunt Silvia down.

It was true that she and Larry had an unfortunate sentimental history, but she was sure he would overlook that.

She'd had no desire for a two-night stand. One night had been enough. She and Larry had avoided each other ever since that disastrous date when he'd tried and failed to stuff what felt like a marshmallow inside her, and they both ended up staring at the ceiling.

That was nothing compared to what was at stake. Her main worry was how to help Silvia right now. How to get her to a safe place and then get her back to the States. She had no idea what to do, who to turn to.

Then she thought of Max. Of course! He was a former SEAL. He'd know what to do, or at least who to contact. The legal implications were something she could think about later, but right now, the most important thing was to keep Silvia safe. Surely he'd know how to do that?

His cell phone number was programmed into hers. She felt a huge surge of relief as she pulled out her phone, checking her watch. 5:00 pm. He'd be on the road. It was dangerous to call someone while they were driving. A text message would be better. It gave off a signal, and he could choose to pull over to the side, and then they could talk.

The message was simple.

SOS – P

There. She felt better already.

He'd help her, and he'd know what to do. Together they'd figure out a way to save Silvia. Now she needed to put that file in a safer place. Where? Max had given her his cell phone but not his email address.

If there was a conspiracy inside the company, who to trust? It was entirely possible that people in the upper echelons knew the truth, and frankly, Paige didn't trust any of them.

There seemed to be a career point above which science started mattering less than profits.

She'd send the file to Larry and to . . . the police? It was a police matter, but no one was hurt . . . yet. The FBI? Silvia had mentioned the FBI. That made sense. Certainly the FBI would know what to do, who to turn to. There must be an FBI office in San Francisco. She logged on to the FBI.gov site and found the link to the San Francisco office, copied the address, and opened her Gmail account.

The drumbeat of anxiety over Silvia's fate was beating in her head as she typed. Max sensed her anxiety and scrunched close to her, leaning against her leg and laying his muzzle across her feet. He always sensed when she was upset.

Paige dropped a hand to briefly scratch his head, then bent back over the keyboard.

Suddenly, to her astonishment Max scrambled to his feet, hunching his shoulders and growling low in his throat.

"Get your hands off that computer," a male voice said.

Paige whipped around, wide-eyed. Two men were in the doorway, one tall and thin, the other stocky and shorter. The tall one had a gun pointed straight at her. She froze, utterly incapable of movement, trying to process these two men who'd appeared from nowhere.

"I said, hands off the fucking keyboard!"

She jerked her trembling hands up as if the keys were on fire. Oh, God! What now? Another minute or two and she could have sent the file to the FBI and to Larry. As it was, the only copies of Silvia's file were on her hard drive and her thumb drive.

The two men came forward. The man with the gun kept it trained on her. The unarmed man came around to stand beside her. He bent forward to see the screen, and Paige got a horrifying whiff of sweat, suntan lotion, and some awful cologne. Instinctively she recoiled when he lowered his head to hers.

Max's growling grew louder, lips curled back from his teeth.

The man tapped the keyboard, closing her FBI search, checking her email history. "Okay," the man said over his shoulder to his armed partner. "This hasn't been forwarded. There's a copy on her hard drive. Deleting . . . now."

"No!" Without thinking, Paige batted his hands away. He gave her a casual backhanded blow that nearly toppled her out of her chair.

Max attacked.

Max, her joyous, friendly dog—barely out of puppyhood— snarled like a hellhound and leaped for the man's throat.

An attacking dog is a fearful thing, like a primal nightmare hurtling out from the darkness. The man shot an arm up to protect his face and stumbled back, giving a high-pitched scream. "Shoot! Shoot the fucking dog, goddamn it!" he shouted.

Paige's head was still woozy from the blow, but when she saw the armed man raise his hand with the gun in it, she screamed and launched herself at him just as he pulled the trigger. The report was loud in the room, stunning her.

Max gave a loud, pained yelp and fell in a boneless heap to the ground, red staining his head.

Paige went wild, shrieking with rage, clawing for the gunman's eyes, feeling flesh under her fingers.

This time the blow was harder, knocking her to the floor next to Max. The world turned black for just a second, then slowly came back into focus. She looked up from the floor at the two men, one holding a red-stained forearm and the other with the gun glaring at her, the two long scratches on his face sullenly bleeding.

Good! she thought viciously, wishing she and Max had inflicted more damage. She reached out blindly and gathered Max into her arms, burying her hands and face in his fur, tears seeping out of her eyes. *Oh God, Max.* Her faithful friend, her . . . she stilled. There was something . . . a faint throbbing under her fingertips.

Max was alive!

Please, don't let him gain consciousness now, she prayed. The man Max attacked had been terrified. One twitch of Max's paw and they'd finish off the job.

Max was completely limp in her arms, but her gorgeous, smart, loving dog was alive. These monsters hadn't killed him.

Suddenly, she was yanked to her feet with a jerk that almost dislocated her shoulder.

"Come with me," the tall man with the gun said, pulling her after him. In her living room, he pushed her down into an armchair.

She'd never seen these two men before, but she could guess who they were. They looked exactly like every other security moron employed lately by GenPlant. Ill-fitting suits with lumps under their jackets, *check*; dour, dull expressions, *check*; a slight hint of sadism, *check*.

They were here and had pulled a weapon on her. Paige understood very well that this probably meant they weren't expecting her to live to testify against them. More goons just like them had presumably been sent to Argentina to find Silvia, but Silvia had managed to elude their grasp. Paige wasn't going to be so lucky. If she wanted to come out of this alive, she was going to have to think fast.

And if she wasn't going to get out of this alive, someone had to know what happened.

She slipped the thumb drive way down into the cushions of the armchair. If anything happened to her, Max or the police would find it. Maybe in time to save her, maybe not. She might die and Silvia might die, but at least the truth would come out.

The tall man brought out a kitchen chair, turned it around and straddled it, gun hand along the top of the back. His index finger stayed within the trigger guard. It was pointed loosely at her.

"So. What do you know about this Argentina thing?"

"I don't know what you're talking about."

This time the blow came from behind. Unexpected. Hard.

When she opened her eyes again, it took her a moment or two to focus. Her head throbbed.

"Okay, that was dumb of you, and I understand you're not a stupid woman. You've got a PhD. So let me tell you upfront that we can keep this up all night," the tall guy said. "No problem. And we can get real inventive. You're a pretty woman. Smart, too, if you work in a lab. So you can connect the dots. My friend and I, we can do what we want here. No limits. We'll get what we want. The only question is: will it be the easy way or the hard way? Your choice."

His eyes were a pale blue, so lifeless they could have been marbles. There was no mercy in them, no emotion at all, not even the pleasure of someone who liked inflicting pain.

Nothing.

Paige was working hard to stop her trembling. These men were barely above animals. Animals had an instinct for fear, and attacked when they sensed it. So she had to control herself.

If she could keep them talking for just another forty minutes, Max would be here. She couldn't defeat these two men but he could. Even with a busted leg, these two idiots would be no match for him.

"So. We know your friend Silvia Ramirez has been trying to contact you all week."

"And she's escaped you all week, hasn't she?" Paige narrowed her eyes at the men. "You didn't lay a hand on her."

"We will. Don't worry about it, our men down there are good."

Not good enough to capture a woman on her own. Paige didn't say the words, but her expression was clear.

"She hasn't been able to establish contact with you, we

know that. We cut her off every time she got you on the phone."

"You were listening to my calls," Paige breathed. That was how they'd done it. The instant they heard Silvia's voice, they cut the connection. Thank God she'd texted Max! "How long have you been doing that?"

Another slap to the back of her head, softer this time. A smack more than a blow. A little something to establish authority. "We ask the questions here, bitch, not you," the thug behind her growled.

The man with the gun studied her, as if she were a bug under a microscope.

"We deleted the file you received. Did Ramirez send you anything else? Another file? Did you receive anything in the mail?"

Ordinarily Paige was a lousy liar. She hated lying because it gave her cognitive dissonance. She was a scientist. Reality was her field of study. Lies were a distortion of reality, and used up significant amounts of space on her mental hard disk. You had to keep track of lies, remember them, coordinate them. Not worth the effort, she'd always thought.

She didn't have to lie now. Silvia hadn't sent anything else and nothing had arrived in the mail.

Paige looked the tall man straight in the eye without blinking. "No, I didn't receive another file and I haven't received anything in the mail."

He held her gaze for a long moment, then shifted his eyes to the man behind her. "She's telling the truth." He waited a beat. "Ramirez tried to contact you all week. Why?"

Paige told a version of the truth. "Because we're friends."

The tall man narrowed his eyes. "She was on the run, desperate. She wasn't trying to contact you to make a date to meet for drinks. Why was she trying to get in touch? To send the file. Anything else?"

Paige said nothing and his mouth flattened.

"Let's try this another way. What do you do at the company?"

That was easy. No cognitive dissonance there. "I'm a plant geneticist. My main field of study is biolistics. Currently I'm applying the agrobacterium method—known as the 'Gene Gun'—in vivo, for the transformation of monocot species, by shooting genes into plant cell chloroplasts."

Silence.

"We need to take this to the lab," the man behind her said. "The one on the island."

Paige's heart started thumping, a frantic tattoo of panic. They couldn't take her to the main company headquarters labs twenty miles away. It was a huge, bright complex, with thousands of employees coming and going at all hours of the day or night. A place where she was well-known.

No, they meant the other complex. GenPlant Laboratories kept facilities on the small island she could see from her deck. Santo Domingo Island. Certain varieties highly susceptible to unintentional cross-breeding were studied there.

Paige had been there once. It was mostly deserted, the main buildings dedicated to micro-propagation under artificial light, automatically watered. It was a series of concrete bunkers with huge underground facilities and only a few researchers who worked sporadically in labs confined to one wing. There wouldn't be anyone now on a Friday evening.

It was a perfect place to hide a prisoner.

It was a perfect place to kill someone and get rid of the body. Once she was on the island, she was lost.

"No," she said. "You can't go there. Company rules—"

She didn't finish the sentence. Something punched her arm, something covered her head, and blackness descended.

Her last thought was, *Max. Help me.*

CHAPTER SIX

Max found himself whistling in the SUV, coming back from the doctor's visit—never his favorite activity. He'd grown to loathe doctors and nurses and physical therapists over the past year. His lost year. The year of putting himself back together.

Good people, all. Probably. And they *had* put his broken pieces together, there was that. But they had never believed he could go back to the way he was before, and Max found that unacceptable. He'd been a hard man and he was determined to come back even harder, no matter what the medical pukes said.

Fuck 'em if they thought he couldn't do it. If they thought he'd injure himself if he pushed himself harder. Well, by God, he'd pushed himself and come out the other end without causing a permanent injury, like they kept nagging he would.

Even his goddamned bad leg was better. The orthopedic surgeon was surprised. *Whatever it is you're doing,* he said, *keep on doing it.*

Well, Max had every intention of doing it. He was up to a one-mile swim, every day. He'd get up to two miles—and then three—and hit that fucking island that was always just out of reach. It was off-limits, he knew that, some kind of research lab. But his goal was to get close to it and swim back. Six miles. Every day. He could do it. Maybe by the end of the year.

And he had his own physical and mental rehab routine now. He'd swim and then spend the day with that damned dog, throwing Frisbees and laughing. It was impossible to be depressed with that mutt around.

Not to mention the mistress, Paige. Oh yeah. He was really looking forward to spending every evening and every night with Paige.

Because it was entirely possible that sex with Paige Waring was what had improved his leg. God knows it improved everything else. And he had every intention of keeping on doing it, just like the doctor ordered.

That was the reason he was whistling. And the reason he was pushing the speed limit. To get back to her.

Man, one week, and his entire outlook on life had changed. Since Afghanistan it had been one grim, gray day after another. Holding on. Surviving. Getting better one painful inch at a time. Putting one foot in front of the other, and considering it a victory, since it had been touch-and-go as to whether he'd ever walk again when he woke up in Ramstein. Touch-and-go as to whether he'd even have a leg, or so the surgeons told him. The operation to save his leg had taken seventeen hours.

His entire life since he'd been a kid had been aimed at joining the navy and becoming a SEAL. It was all he'd ever wanted. Now that he'd never be a SEAL again, the future had been closed off, this impenetrable black iron wall clanging down right in front of him.

He still didn't know what the long-term future held, but

his immediate future was spending his evenings with gorgeous Paige Waring in her pretty apartment and spending his days with her dog.

Not bad for a man who only a week ago hated the thought of waking up in the morning.

It was sex. That was part of it. Granted, hotter and better sex than he'd ever had, but sex was fleeting. No one knew that better than him.

Up until now, he'd thought sex was fucking. Who knew sex could also be lovemaking? And that lovemaking was *better* than just sex? Though they'd smoked the sheets up, there was affection there. Real, tangible affection. Warmth and connection.

He liked her. A lot. And was beginning, for the first time in his life, to think of the "L" word. Much scarier than "like."

She was smart and funny and just so goddamned pretty. But beyond the prettiness there had been other things he wanted to explore and knew he would. Because now that he'd found this, tasted it, there was no going back.

She kept him on his toes. She made his heart beat faster and his blood boil. And at the same time, he found a strange kind of peace with her, as if he'd come home after a long and weary journey.

It was going to take him a long, long time to grow tired of Paige Waring. Maybe the rest of his life.

The sun was low in the sky, the light washing over the landscape. The effect was spectacular, every color kicked up a notch until it glowed. If he hurried, they could watch the sun set from Paige's deck. Maybe he could coax her into sitting on his lap. Oh yeah. His dick stirred at the thought.

Man, his dick was making up for lost time. No sex at all for two years and now it wouldn't stay down.

But that was okay because it was happy and so was he.

Everything about this moment was just so fucking perfect. Doctors not riding him for overdoing it, for a change. A beautiful woman waiting for him. A ridiculously likeable dog waiting for him, too. A glorious sunset.

When was the last time he looked forward to something? Noticed a beautiful sunset? Noticed fucking *colors*? And when was the last time he'd felt so goddamned *good*?

There was a wonderful evening ahead of him. He'd deliberately had a light lunch because he was looking forward to whatever it was Paige was going to cook for dinner. And then, oh man, spending the night with Paige. Making love until they were sated—or at least she was. Max felt like he could go forever, now that he'd reconnected with his dick. And then sleeping in on a Saturday morning, that slender soft body curled up next to his. And maybe they'd spend all day Sunday in bed.

The future rocked.

He was really looking forward to days playing with her stupid mutt on the beach, waiting for her to come home. Maybe one of these evenings he'd try to rustle up some dinner himself, just for some comic relief. There was a hospital nearby in case it all went south.

Maybe tomorrow evening they could go into Monterey. He could take her out to a nice restaurant, maybe out to a movie. Maybe—what the fuck—maybe dancing? Though he didn't know how to dance and would trip over his own feet, not to mention the bum leg. But she looked like a woman who might like that—dinner and dancing.

And God knows, whatever made her happy was okay by him.

Because, well, she'd given him his life back.

He was . . . he was *happy*. Looking forward to seeing her again. Looking forward to life.

He pulled out his cell and punched in her number. To tell her he was about an hour out. To ask her if she needed him to pick up anything in town.

Who the fuck was he kidding? He just wanted to hear her voice, hear that she was happy he was coming back to her. Hell, maybe hear the sound of that mutt barking in the background.

NO SIGNAL.

Damn. He really wanted to hear her voice. Tell her about the doctor's visit, about the cheeky squirrel staring at him from the branch of a tree outside the clinic while the doctor was bent over his leg.

Shit.

He tried again fifteen minutes later.

NO SIGNAL.

Five minutes later.

NO SIGNAL.

Max drummed his fingers on the steering wheel. Damn but he wanted to hear her voice. Right now. She had this most amazing voice. Soft but clear, just a little husky in bed.

Last night she'd whispered, *"Now, Max"* right into his ear, just as her little cunt started pulling on him, her breath washing over his ear. He'd started moving faster, harder, and it had set her off.

Oh, Christ. *Don't think about that.* Because his entire body had flushed with heat and his cock stirred again at the memory.

It had been like that all day, with a real embarrassing moment on the doctor's cot when he'd remembered her kissing his scars and he'd started getting an erection.

That earned him a real odd look from Dr. McBride, former college linebacker. Max had had to think of Afghanistan to get his cock back down again.

Oh God, he missed her. He wanted to be back in her apartment *now*, on her deck. Petting her dog, sipping a glass of wine with her. Watching this spectacular sunset. Right now. Right . . . fucking . . . now.

The cell phone's buzz startled him. The signal was back.

A text message. He glanced at the display. It was from Paige. Not only was her number memorized on his SIM card, it was emblazed in his head.

His blood stopped cold when he saw the message.

SOS - P.

Fuck. She was in trouble.

Max stepped hard on the accelerator.

A loud, angry buzzing filled her head, the ground underneath her thumping up and down. She bounced each time, coming down jarringly hard on a wooden surface that had knobs and lumps on it. It hurt. Her arm hurt. Everything hurt, particularly her head. It felt as if someone were hammering spikes into her skull.

She tried to cushion the bounces but her hands wouldn't

move. Was she paralyzed? No, her fingers could move, but her hands couldn't.

It was impossible to think with this loud buzzing noise, the jarring motions rolling her back and forth and up and down. Sometimes the ground beneath her suddenly dropped and she fell with a painful jolt.

It was dark, but bright pinpricks of light came through.

None of this made any sense. Where was she? What—

And then it all came back in a sickening, painful rush. The two men. Max, shot and bleeding. Silvia, on the run. The file Silvia had sent, with the terrible data.

She was lying on her side, hooded, her hands in restraints, totally unable to counter the painful jolts.

Men's voices over the deep buzzing noise. An engine. A boat engine. The smell of brine penetrating the smelly material of her hood. She was on a boat with those two men. They were taking her to Santo Domingo.

She surreptitiously tried to see if her cell phone was still in her pants pocket. If it was, she could be traced through it. A sudden surge of hope pulsed through her as she rolled with the rolling of the boat, trying to bring her wrists around to touch her pockets.

Nothing. Her cell phone was gone. Whether they'd thrown it away or left it behind in her apartment, it was of no use to her.

The deep buzzing of the engine changed tone, lowered. The boat swung sideways. They were landing.

She breathed through the sudden panic. Once she was on that island, she was lost. No one could find her—not even Max, even if he knew where she was. The facility had over fifty thousand square feet of research labs, culture labs, propagation houses, and equipment sheds, plus a huge hangar-like building called the Repository, a bank of varieties for future testing.

There'd be plenty of privacy. No one would hear her screaming. The two men could do to her what they wanted, with no one the wiser.

For all anyone knew, she would disappear off the face of the earth.

She could only hope that Max had found the thumb drive. But even if he did, how could he know where they had taken her?

The boat's engine cut and it rocked gently on the water. A strong hand wrapped itself around her upper arm and pulled sharply, taking her by surprise. She'd been planning on pretending to still be unconscious but when he pulled her stumblingly upright, she automatically scrambled to find her footing.

One of the men was at her back and prodded her roughly onto a plank. At the end, unmistakeably, was solid ground.

She was on the island.

And she was lost.

CHAPTER SEVEN

"Paige!" Max pounded on the door with his fist. "Paige, open up!"

There was no sound. No quick footsteps, no voice, nothing.

Max raised his fist again, then brought it quietly to rest against the door. He rested his forehead against it, disgusted at himself.

Shit. He was a SEAL. He'd trained for years. This was not how to stage an infiltration. What the fuck was the matter with him? He knew better than this.

There was no way of knowing what that SOS message meant, but one thing was certain—Paige needed him. If she was in real trouble, if someone was holding her hostage on the other side of that door, he'd just thrown away every single tactical advantage he had. Just wiped it out.

If there was someone behind that door, that someone now knew that an angry male was on the other side. He could hurt Paige, kill her.

Max broke out in sweat. Maxwell Wright, whose heart rate never increased in battle, was sweating like a pig, the sweat of anxiety. Super-cool SEAL, tested and tried in the battlefield. He was good in combat, he had the medals to prove it.

Now look at him. Sweating, panicky, ready to barge into a dangerous, unknown situation—which ran counter to every single thing he'd ever been taught. Any instructor worth his salt would have kicked his ass.

He knew better than this. He had to do better than this. Paige needed him. Whatever was wrong, a quiet, controlled response was better than a sweaty, panicked one, hands down.

If his drill instructor had just seen him, he'd have screamed in his face and told him to drop to the grinder and pump out a hundred push-ups.

Intel. He needed intel.

He stood an inch from the door, breathing hard, staving off panic. *Think! Goddamn it!*

The bottom rim of the huge, golden red sun was close to touching the surface of the sea. The air was filled with golden light, but in an hour it would be dusk, the light gray and unrevealing. Whatever he learned here, it had to be now, with the light.

Carefully, he made his way around the perimeter of the house. It had the exact same layout as his own. Living room with adjoining kitchen, hallway with two rooms and a bathroom. When he reached the study window, he heard a whine, looked in.

Max! Max huddled on the floor in a pool of blood. The dog raised his blood-streaked head when he saw him and gave a half-hearted bark.

Now he was certain that there was no one in the house—otherwise, even wounded as he was, Max would be barking harder.

Max went back to the front door and froze. How the fuck had he missed this? He had to get his act together because he'd missed what he should have seen right off, if he hadn't been crazy with fear for Paige.

Scratches on the backplate. Paige's front door lock had been picked.

Evidence, right there, that someone had come for Paige. Was holding her somewhere, right now. Could be hurting her, right this minute.

The panic dissolved and icy calm took its place. Years of training steadied him, gave him the right place in his head to go to. A place of discipline and training and determination.

Once Max entered that place, he was invincible. It would take an RPG to take him down.

He had the key to Paige's place. A minute later, he was in the house, bending down to the dog.

"Good boy," he said soothingly, touching Max's head. Max whined once when he touched the open wound. A furrow, caused by a bullet. Max licked his hand as he studied the wound. It was only a flesh wound. It had bled a lot, but the bleeding had stopped.

Max went into the bathroom, got a towel and disinfectant, and carefully cleaned the shallow wound as best he could. The dog licked his hand. "It's okay, boy. You'll be okay." The furry tail thumped once on the floor.

Max noticed blood on the muzzle, unconnected to the head wound.

Oh, yeah. Good for him.

"Bit the fucker, did you, Max? Good boy. You're the best. I hope you tore his fucking throat out." But looking around, he saw that, besides a few drops of blood near Paige's desk, no one's throat had been ripped out.

Well, that could be remedied.

"Where'd they take her, boy? Where's Paige?"

Astonishingly, Max rose unsteadily to his feet. He stumbled, fell. Before Max could reach down to pet him, reassure him, the dog rose again and stood.

He was standing, though he must have been weak from blood loss. He was standing, though in all likelihood he was lightly concussed. He was hurt, but, by God, he was standing.

He was as brave as any SEAL.

"Where's Paige?" Max said again, feeling like an idiot. The dog was smart, but not that smart.

To his surprise, though, the dog moved slowly, painfully into the living room, stopping at a flower- covered armchair. Max followed.

Now that he'd calmed down, Max could read the situation in front of him as clearly as if seeing what had happened an hour or so ago. There were two chairs dragged in from the kitchen, one in front of the armchair, one sitting right behind it. Two men, then, flanking Paige. The seat of the armchair was still dented where she'd sat.

He looked more closely. There was something about the crease on the left hand side of the big seat cushion, corresponding to Paige's right hand. He dug and came out with something small and metallic.

A thumb drive.

Smart, smart Paige. She'd had the presence of mind under threat to leave him something. What? He was distracted by Max. The dog's coordination was improving by the minute. He was trotting back and forth between where Max sat in front of Paige's computer and the front door, whining, pointing his nose at the door, clearly exasperated with the human Max who wasn't getting it.

Paige went out this door, Max was communicating with every fiber of his doggy being. *What's the matter with you, you moron? Come on, let's go get her!*

But human Max needed more intel. Going blind into a situation was not good. Max stared at the screen, willing himself to understand what Paige wanted him to know.

He scrolled briefly through a couple of files randomly. All work related. When he opened them he simply stared, understanding one word in ten. Some were data spreadsheets. Some were graphs. Some lab results. The physics and genetics and biochemistry were way beyond him.

OK. He'd stand in awe of her education some other time. Right now he needed to know what was in here that could help him find her, and fast.

When he'd gone over the files three times—fending off Max, who was scrabbling at his leg and whining loudly—he decided to look at them in chronological order, something he should have done immediately.

The first one—Christ! It had been loaded less than an hour ago. Maybe the last thing she did before the two fucks picked her lock, shot her dog, and spirited her away.

He finally clicked through and saw a personal message, which he'd missed in his scrolling. From a woman named Silvia, who was apparently a friend. He read through the message and finally reached a grim understanding.

The company Paige worked for was sitting on a bomb that

was about to blow up in its face. A bomb that, at a conservative estimate, was about to cost them millions, maybe billions. Something like this would eventually come out, but from what Max was able to see, right now the only thing standing between the bomb and the world was two super-smart women. One was being chased all over Argentina and the other had been kidnapped.

He opened his cell, engaged an encryption app designed by the friend he was calling, and waited.

"Yo. World's Finest Hacker. Black Hat, White Hat, take your pick. How may I help you?"

Oh yeah. Cory Mayer, former Delta operator. Max had met him on a cross-training exercise. Cory had been a gifted shooter, but it turned out he was even more gifted with a keyboard, which had turned out handy when an IED had exploded under his badly-armored vehicle outside Nasiriyah seven years ago. He'd left his legs back in Iraq—but not his brains. He'd since recycled to become everyone's go-to guy for intel.

"Yo, Hackerman. I've got myself a time-sensitive situation here. A possible kidnap victim, works for GenPlant Laboratories. What can you tell me about the company?"

"Hm. How you been, Maxie boy? You getting over your scratches?"

Max nearly smiled. Though Cory's voice was slow and honeyed he could hear wild tapping in the background.

"Doing fine now, except for this woman. She works for the company, does research work for them. I think she's come across some information that will hurt the company."

"Oh ho!" Cory chortled. "Are we talking babe material, here?"

"Yeah," Max said curtly. "And it's a woman I care about. A lot."

There was silence at the other end, but the pounding sounds intensified.

"Okay." When he came back online, Cory's voice was curt and serious. "Here's what we've got. Big company, last year's profits were half a billion dollars on three billion sales. Has come up with some killer apps—two new types of antibiotics that can overcome resistant e. coli infections and pesticide-resistant fruit trees. And that was just last year. Seems to be humming right along."

Okay. "It's got research facilities in Argentina. What can you tell me about that?"

Another minute as Cory worked his magic. "Yep. A big research facility four hundred miles south of Buenos Aires."

"Anything wonky there?"

"Not that I can see."

Max knew there was but it was clearly still hidden. Not even Cory, brilliant as he was, could see things that weren't there yet.

"How about their security?"

After a minute, Cory said, "Oh."

"What? What?"

"Not good. Someone's been hiring from Magnum Secure lately. Hiring heavily. I'd say now a good 70 percent of their security staff comes from there. Bad juju, Max."

Very bad juju. Magnum Secure was a notoriously corrupt private contractor that had operated extensively in the Sandbox. He'd come across MS operators a lot, and they were aggressive and greedy. The owner seemed to recruit men who cared for nothing but the bottom line. If someone in Paige's company had been filling its security department with ex-MS contractors, Paige was in trouble.

None of the operators would draw the line at hurting a woman.

"The woman in question's name is Paige Waring, Cory. Like I said, she's a researcher there. I'm at her house now and there are signs of a struggle. I think she's been kidnapped because she holds some information about something that went wrong at their lab in Argentina. Where do you think they'd take her? To headquarters? It's about twenty miles from here."

"Pulling up satellite images now . . . no. I don't think so. It's a busy facility. There's a huge parking lot with cars going in and out constantly. My images are from fifteen minutes ago and there's a lot of movement. Dunno, Max, just seems too public for a kidnapping. I can't even see any outbuildings where someone could be held."

The dog's whining was stronger now, with a note of urgency in it. He was pawing Max's leg. The dog went back to the front door, looking over his shoulder at Max, and barked.

Was Paige being held nearby? Is that what Max was trying to tell him?

"Listen," he told Cory. "I gotta see about something. Can you send those images to my Gmail account and we'll talk in five? And see if you can find any databases with other property the corporation might own nearby."

"Sure thing," Cory said. "A woman, huh?"

"Yeah. Smart and kind and pretty. Exactly the kind of woman fuckheads like to hurt."

Max could almost hear Cory's teeth grinding. His mom had been beaten to death by his dad. He was guaranteed to give Max his best.

Max opened the front door and the dog flowed out, nose to the ground. To Max's astonishment, instead of making a grid back and forth to try to pick up Paige's scent, the dog ran around the house and headed straight for the beach.

What the fuck?

He'd been prepared for Max to lose the scent right away. They'd have driven her away in a car. When Max headed for the beach, nose still to the ground, his heart sank. Sweat broke out in every pore.

Had they killed Paige and buried her on the beach? Their stretch of beach was usually deserted. The beach narrowed along their stretch and the bed was rocky. The popular beach was two miles down—long wide stretches of sand and no rocks underfoot.

Oh God, now he could see it, as plain as day. Three sets of footprints, two on either side of deeply furrowed tracks. Two men holding up an unconscious woman. Then halfway down the beach, two sets of footprints, one much deeper than the other. The depth of a man carrying an adult woman.

Max had followed his nose straight to the water, so at least he wasn't going to find Paige's body in a shallow grave. The dog was at the water's edge, moving back and forth anxiously, unable to follow the scent into the sea. The sea that might contain Paige's body.

Max rejected that idea violently. Shook it right the hell off. He'd just found her, he wasn't going to lose her. Not an option.

Coming closer to the water the footprints were muddled. And there was a long indentation in the sand, with a heavy furrow in the middle. The kind of print a boat with a hull would make.

He refused to even think that they were putting Paige on the boat to dump her overboard. It was still daylight. Would they risk someone seeing them on open water when there were other, easier options available? Why put Paige in a boat? Ten miles east and you could get onto the largest freeway system in the world and disappear.

They had to keep her alive for a reason. And they put her on a boat for a reason.

Max was going to find her and hurt the men who'd taken her, and then he was going to bring her home. That was his mission and he hadn't failed a mission yet.

"Max!" he called and slapped his thigh. The dog looked up from where he was nosing the sand, completely recovered and quivering with anxiety. "Come with me!"

The dog hesitated, torn. He wanted to stay where there was the last sign of his mistress, but she wasn't there. On the other hand, maybe the male human could help. He slowly trotted to him.

Max headed for his apartment because he knew Mel would have everything he could possibly need. He needed speed because someone could be hurting Paige right now. He nearly ran back, ignoring the grinding pain in his leg.

Mel had security cameras front and back, something Paige didn't but would have—just as soon as Max got her back. He'd install security cameras right away, alarms at the doors and windows and fence, and front and back door electronic security systems not even he could penetrate.

Mel's cameras worked on a forty-eight-hour loop and they were digital, hi-def cameras. So when Max moved the tape back, he watched, every muscle in his body tensed, as three men drove up in a tan SUV. Two men got out, one stayed in the car.

Max watched as the taller of the two men picked Paige's lock and they walked in. He fast-forwarded to when the two men walked out, dragging a semi-conscious, hooded Paige.

They stopped at the SUV to talk to the driver who backed the SUV and drove away.

While they were talking, the camera caught the faces of all three men. Max froze the camera, studying the three men carefully, knowing he would never forget those faces—they were dead men walking.

He flipped open his cell and called Cory back. He didn't even have a chance to say anything when Cory said, excitedly, "Max, GenPlant Labs has a super-secret facility on an island not far from where you are now. The island is called—"

"Santo Domingo Island, yeah. Listen, do you think there's any chance of satellite coverage of the island? Say, from about an hour ago to now? Can you hack Keyhole?"

He knew what he was asking. Keyhole was the NSA's top-secret series of eyes in the sky so powerful they could see the balls of flies. Keyhole intel was beamed down in code so highly encrypted it took a bank of servers to decode.

But Cory was a genius.

"Please," Cory said. "For you, anything. But I'll do you one better. There's a big oil consortium looking for shale oil via a new imaging technology. They've covered all of Central California with something like four thousand bird-sized drones. Each drone records a tiny area and a computer puts a composite picture together. That picture would be much clearer than Keyhole."

Max didn't even question how Cory could know that. And didn't bother asking Cory to hack into the central computer putting together the mosaic of drone photograms. He could hear Cory pounding the keyboard. Cory knew what to look for.

Five minutes later, Cory whistled.

"What?"

Cory's voice was grim. "Not looking good, big guy. I'll send these images to your cell. I'm looking at a boat that landed on a pier on the south side of the island at 17:47. The time stamp will be on the footage. Then we see two guys pulling out what looks like a hooded female—she's stumbling and they're dragging her along . . ."

Max could picture it all too well, the two men who'd been on the security footage manhandling Paige. His hands fisted.

"You're going to get these fuckers, correct, Max?" Cory asked. "They're really manhandling her." For a moment, all Max could hear was Cory's rough breathing. "One of those fuckers just backhanded her. She fell to the ground. God*damn* it!"

Max closed his eyes and grappled for control. "Oh, yeah," he said softly. "I'm going to get them. Count on it."

"Good. I'm watching them disappear into the main building. Straight up from the jetty. The good news is that they entered the building through what looks like the front door, so we know where she was at 17:54. The bad news is that the central building is enormous. There are several outbuildings, and we have no way of telling if there are underground corridors. No way of knowing where she might be now."

If she's still alive. Cory didn't say it but it hung there in the air.

Max wasn't going there. Not touching it. "What can you tell me about the island? How many people are on it—can you tell?"

"It's hard to say. There are no cars, of course. There's a jetty on the south side, but only for small boats. That's where they landed. I can't imagine boats carrying much more than ten people mooring there. Hang on, wait a minute. Let me check." Max held his cell to his ear, clutching it so hard it was a miracle the plastic didn't break.

The urge to spring into action was so strong it prickled under his skin but he knew better than to be impatient at the planning stage. Paige was in danger, but she wouldn't be helped by him barging in unprepared and getting his ass capped.

"Okay." Cory came back online. "There are two guards stationed on the north side of the facility. And two more at the jetty. I went back in time to check their routine and they patrol every half hour, fifteen minutes to each quadrant. They're armed—looks like AK-74 rifles. Sidearms, too, but they're holstered and I don't have enough resolution to tell what they are. They stick close to the buildings. If that's a normal research facility I'll French-kiss you."

Max nearly smiled. "Thanks, buddy, I'll pass."

"No way to know how many people are inside or where they're holding your friend. Sorry. The drones don't have IR capability. That's going to come online next month, or so I heard. But right now what's under the roofs is unknowable. And it'll be dark soon."

"Yeah. I better get going. Thanks. I owe you."

"Just bring that woman back safely. Check your cell, you'll see the images. I'll be on standby. Let me know if I can help with anything. And don't forget my buddy PJ. Pretty high up in the SF FBI office."

"Yeah. Listen. I'm going to send you a file. Forward it to PJ."

"Got it."

"You're the best."

"Yes, I am. Bring her home, Max."

"You bet. Count on it."

Max carefully studied the images Cory sent him, then went to Mel's locker, where he knew he would find everything he needed. Mel had given him the combination, and sure enough, it was full of gear.

The right gear, bless Mel's black heart.

As in all missions, Max had to balance out gear and weight. Too little gear was bad, too much gear was bad. It had to be Goldilocks Gear, just right. His hands were already picking things out.

Mel had a sweet little suppressed MP-5 that felt like home in his hands. He picked up a Glock 45 and holster as backup. Three magazines each. Night vision binocs. Emerson folder. Four flashbangs. Restraints and duct tape. Waterproof bag. Wet suit and tanks.

Some C-4, det cord and detonator—because there were few situations where blowing something up didn't help.

He went out onto his deck and checked the island with Mel's powerful x140 binoculars, running a slow, careful sweep east to west, then west to east. He saw the jetty with a small boat moored there. Two guards were standing together about fifty feet away. One was smoking. They had their backs to the ocean.

Sloppy. Real sloppy. If he survived the swim, he could take them down easy.

He was deliberate in his actions, not hurrying, though the drumbeat of fear and rage was in his ears. He gave one last long, slow look at the island, at where his Paige was being held, then put on his wet suit. He checked it, checked the tanks, though he knew it wouldn't be in Mel's locker if it wasn't in perfect shape. Force of habit from a man whose life had always depended on the trustworthiness of his gear.

Time to go.

He stepped down from the deck onto the sand, but stopped when he heard a bark. Max on the deck, watching him. To his dying day, Max would swear the dog looked at him with reproachful eyes.

It was crazy, and it would make his task—already nearly impossible—harder. But he was going to have to search a huge building for Paige, with no idea how to track her. Max could be invaluable.

"You want to help me, big boy?"

Max whined and trembled with eagerness.

He went back into the house, dropping a hand to Max's head to scratch behind his ears. "OK, boy. We're going to go get her together. We're a team."

Mel's locker had a small inflatable dinghy, something he probably used when the grandkids came. It took only a few minutes to inflate.

At the beach, he watched Max. The dog bent to track his mistress, nose rooting around the sand, stopping at the water's edge, then looking back up at him.

He pointed. "In." Max leaped into the inflatable.

He looked at the dog, the friendliest mutt on the face of the earth up until about two hours ago. Now, with blood on the side of his head from a bullet and blood on his muzzle from having mauled a man in defense of his mistress, Paige's dog stared up at him with cold, determined eyes. A warrior.

Yessir.

That made two of them.

Man and dog looked out to the island, to where the woman they both loved was being held captive.

It was three miles away. Nothing, in his SEAL days. One of their training exercises back in the day was being dropped ten miles from shore and having to swim back.

But since coming back from the dead, Max had never been able to swim more than a mile. Even that was stretching it. He'd stop in the water, cold and exhausted, knowing if he went any further he'd never make it back in.

This was three.

Towing a small inflatable with thirty pounds of gear and forty pounds of dog.

He shifted his weight onto his good leg. The bad one was aching, shooting messages of pain which he ignored.

The sun was huge, red, glimmering, halfway into the ocean. Soon it would be completely submerged, giving way to night.

Time to go.

"Let's go get Paige, Max," he said, pushing the inflatable into the water. The dog answered with a short bark.

He put on his fins, adjusted his face mask, and slipped under the surface, clutching the tow rope. Going after his woman and prepared to die in the attempt.

Hoo-yah.

CHAPTER EIGHT

Paige sat in a chair in a large empty room. Most of the room was in darkness, the only illumination coming from the big ceiling light directly above her.

At one point it had been a propagation lab. The room still had trestle tables set up for the exacting work, but everything else was gone except for a few chairs. For the first half hour after they'd pushed her into this room and taped her to the chair, she'd desperately tried to free herself. But all she managed to do was tire herself out and make her headache worse.

Each time the iron legs of the chair scraped against the concrete floor, the sound echoed in the room. However hard she wrenched, the tape held. Wrists and ankles bound with duct tape, she was also bound to the chair, the tape wrapped around her waist, thighs, and shins.

In her desperate attempt to free herself, she'd almost tipped over. She stopped immediately. Being bound to a tipped over chair, unable to move, would be even worse than her current situation, not to mention the fact that if she fell wrong, she could knock herself out. Whatever was coming, she had to keep her wits about her to deal with it.

So she stilled and tried to reason her way out of this situation.

The problem was, she had so few data. She had an analytical mind, but it needed facts to work with.

Fact: Silvia had stumbled upon a terrible side effect of a GenPlant experiment. Paige knew that the company wasn't a corrupt fly-by-night operation. It would halt the experiments immediately. But obviously someone in the company wasn't so honourable and had hired goons to back him up in a rogue operation to keep the experiment going.

Fact: she had no idea who that was, though if she had to bet, her money would be on Jonathan Finder.

Fact: She had no idea what had happened to Silvia, or if she was even alive.

Fact: she had no idea what was going to happen to her.

Fact: Max would come for her. It wasn't a wish, it was truth. Something about the past week they'd passed together had given her that certainty. He'd come for her as fast as he could, but he had no idea where she was. Now she regretted bitterly not talking to him about her worries over Silvia.

Why hadn't she? He wasn't a good-time boyfriend, there for laughter and sex, gone with the wind when there were problems. Everything she knew about him told her that.

She could have told him, and with hindsight should have told him, but . . . this past week had been so wonderful, so extraordinary, that she'd instinctively kept the world at bay to create a little bubble for them.

How wrong she'd been.

He'd have found her dog by now. Paige hoped with all her heart that he'd found a wounded Max and not a dead Max, but he'd understand that something violent had happened. He was probably calling hospitals in the area, maybe involving the police. But there would be no clues. Even if he found her thumb drive, it wouldn't have any concrete clues.

It seemed like hours went by and no one came for her. She simply sat, bound to a chair, trying not to panic. She had no wristwatch and no cell phone and no way to judge the time passing.

Were there guards posted outside the door? Even if there weren't, she couldn't move. And even if, by some miracle, she were able to free herself and evade the men who'd brought her here, she was trapped on an island. There was no way she could swim back to shore. It must be three miles. She'd die trying to escape.

She tried to calm herself with yoga breathing exercises but they weren't working. Her heart pounded fast and heavy. It was hard to breathe, as if something were crushing her chest.

Footsteps sounded outside and she straightened, heart rate doubling, sweat breaking out on her back.

Across the big room, the steel door unlocked with a snick and slowly opened. Paige tensed, breath caught in her lungs.

A man slowly walked into the room, identity unclear in the murky light. He stepped into the cone of light and Paige slumped in relief. Larry Pelton.

"Larry! Oh, thank God!" She wrestled one last time with the duct tape. "Get these things off me! Two men who work for GenPlant kidnapped me and they're after Silvia, too. We have to hurry!"

Larry walked up to her, reached out a hand. At first she thought he was going to rip the duct tape but he didn't have a knife. The only person she could imagine ripping that tape with his bare hands was Max, and Larry was no Max.

Instead, he put his finger to her throat and watched as his hand drifted down to the first button of her shirt.

"So pretty," he mused.

Paige was so shocked she didn't move as his hand slid into her shirt and cupped her breast. He leaned down and with his other hand grabbed the hair at the back of her head so she couldn't move, and kissed her.

Larry Pelton had been one of the world's monumentally bad kissers. Epically bad. She often thought, during their very brief liaison, that he should have his kissing license taken away. His tongue slipped into her mouth like a warm slug, retreating before she could bite him.

The door opened again and two men came in. Two armed men. The men who'd kidnapped her.

Larry smiled as he lifted his head, fisted hand in her hair tugging so hard it hurt. "Paige, my dear." He shook his head in sadness. "You and your friend Silvia have been giving me so much grief. It's going to be a real pleasure making you pay."

During Hell Week—132 hours of continuous torture—Max ran two hundred miles in combat boots and full combat gear, swam fifty miles, did a thousand push-ups, and endured hours and hours of surf torture, all on four hours' sleep. It was so grueling 70 percent of the candidates rang the bell before day two.

He did it by refusing to quit.

Simply refusing. He'd rather die.

By the end of the week he was in constant pain, and when Hell Week was over on Friday afternoon, he collapsed where he stood. At the medical exam, he had shin splints and four torn ligaments. The doctor had simply looked at him, patted his shoulder and said quietly, "Good job."

No one was going to pat his back now. It didn't make any difference because what was waiting at the other end was much more valuable than his Budweiser.

Paige.

A living Paige. Laughing in his arms.

He could face the future, even a future outside the Teams, if he had her by his side. The thought of living without Paige in his world terrified him. It would be like having all the lights switched off and living in darkness for the rest of his life.

If he had to swim to hell and back for her, he would, gladly.

He paced himself, knowing he couldn't use his combat swim technique, which was fast and powerful. He simply didn't have the strength or the stamina. Max had trained all his adult life and he knew his body intimately. At his peak, he could almost guarantee that as far and as fast as a human could swim, that's how far and how fast he could.

But he'd come close to death. His injuries had been deep and grievous. He'd lost forty pounds of muscle and hadn't put it all back. Thinking he'd power his way to Paige was a good way to kill himself.

The thought was grinding and humiliating, but if he had any chance of surviving this, he had to do it the smart way.

His strokes were slow to conserve power, using his arms more than his legs because his left leg was almost useless.

He swam, tugging the tiny rubber boat with Max and his gear in it, emptying his mind of everything but the will to get to the island.

He surfaced for a second to get his bearings. His injured leg couldn't kick as hard and it threw him off course.

That was what he told himself, but the truth was he was reaching the limits of his strength. And he was only a third of the way there.

It was almost night, though there was just enough pewter in the sky to clearly see the island, a dark triangular shape in the distance.

Max clung to the side of the inflatable, breathing deeply, staring at the island. He glanced at his hand holding onto the tug rope. It was shaking.

The dog made a soft whining sound, shifted slightly to bring his muzzle close, and licked his hand. The dog wanted Paige back as much as he did. He was wounded—he'd been shot in the head—and yet he was unwavering. He'd jumped into the inflatable without hesitation and had remained utterly still while, underwater, Max towed him. Dogs don't have good eyesight; the way they make sense of their world is through their noses.

For the dog, Max had suddenly disappeared, and the inflatable dinghy with the uncertain footing simply began moving. It must have been terrifying, but Max saw no signs of fear in the dog, only determination.

He looked down at his hand. The trembling had stopped.

He had his team. He had his mission.

Go.

He slipped under the water again.

"You weren't very helpful to my men," Larry said casually. He'd brought a chair to sit down on, not straddling it like the goon had done back at her house, but sitting down properly, one elegantly-clad leg over the other. "They told me. That's why you're here." He *tssked*. "You made me come all the way over here when it really wasn't necessary, Paige."

The hair stood up all over her body and she realized, in a single swooping sensation, that the two men had had orders to kill her. She hadn't given them what they wanted and they'd understood they didn't have the technical knowledge to grill her, so they'd just grabbed her and carted her here.

The facility was deserted.

Larry could do what he wanted.

Her life was quite unmistakeably on the line.

"So, Paige. Let's have our little talk now." He shot back a cuff and checked his wristwatch. A Patek Philippe, because Larry liked his stuff. "My men in Buenos Aires should be calling at any moment to say they've got Silvia. When we've wrapped things up here, I can consider this entire episode closed."

"Are you crazy?" Paige asked, then clenched her jaw. Antagonizing Larry was not smart right now. She made her voice reasonable. "Think it through, Larry. The data Silvia has is un-official, yes, but it's hard data. HGHM-1 is a massive failure and will be shut down the instant the news is out. You can't hide something like this forever."

Larry smiled, the smile of a parent listening to a young child explaining the tooth fairy. "It doesn't need to be forever, my dear. There is an end point to this. HGHM-1 is officially a success. News of the fantastic test results will leak tomorrow. GenPlant stocks will soar. My broker is going to leak the news and says the share price will probably increase tenfold. Nowadays it's really hard to find good investments. Money will pour in. I've bought a hundred-thousand shares in the company worth a million bucks, a lot of it on spec. Multiply by ten and you've got a cool ten mil, in a week."

Paige stared at him, frowning. "But—but it's *not* a success. Even if—" she swallowed. "Even if you get rid of us and bury Silvia's data, it will come out sooner rather than later. The figures I saw speak for themselves. Anyone in the company would recognize them and close HGHM-1 right down. It's just a question of time."

As she spoke, a sense of relief washed through her. There was no incentive, really, in killing them because there'd be no stopping the process. Killing them would bring him nothing—expose him to huge risk—and that was her best defense.

"Ah, my dear," Larry said, smiling. "All I need is just a little time. When news leaks out, as it will starting tomorrow—and the share price goes through the roof—I'm going to sell at the top and bail. There's a job waiting for me at Laster Labs. New job, new life, over ten million stashed safely in Aruba. Life's a bowl of cherries, sweetheart."

She shook her head. "It's not that easy. When the shares tank, as they will, as they must, they're going to look carefully at all employees who bought and sold big blocks of shares. Insider trading is a federal offense, and—"

"Ah, ah, Paige, my dear." Larry shook his head. "I'm not stupid. My broker split the purchase up into fictitious accounts, staggered so that there's no suspicion. My broker also fronted me the money to organize this—" With a flick of his wrist he included the two thugs behind him. "What do soldiers call it? This *op*." His lips pursed around the word and made a slight smacking sound on the "p".

Paige's head fell back. "You *are* crazy."

His smile grew. "Not at all. Sane as they come, and soon to be filthy rich."

She looked at him carefully, in his casual, expensive clothes. Closely shaven, pricey haircut, fabulous shoes. It would be nice to think that the monster in him showed, but it didn't. His eyes were twinkling, a half smile on his face. As a matter of fact, he looked exactly the way he had looked at a company mixer when he'd attracted her enough for her to accept a date.

He looked perfectly ordinary. There was absolutely no way to tell that he was willing to kill two people—maybe more—or to let an experiment gone terribly bad continue and have her dog shot, all for money.

"So. Let us begin." He looked down at his neatly pressed trousers and flicked at an imaginary piece of dust, then looked back up at her, suddenly serious. He blinked, blue eyes pale and empty. And *now* Paige could see the monster in him. "Paige. My dear. Where is your dear friend Silvia?"

"I don't know."

She saw the blow coming but was unable to avoid it, was only able to brace for it.

Larry drew back his fist, punched her on the side of the head, and sent her crashing to the floor.

"Wrong answer, bitch."

CHAPTER NINE

Afterwards, Max would have little recollection of swimming to the shore of the island, just one long period of pain and exhaustion while wet. Just like Hell Week, which was a painful blur in his mind, punctuated by a few memories of extreme pain.

Coming up out of surf torture and running with his swim buddy to the grinder—artillery shells popping, smoke from grenades billowing, confusing them. They hardly needed smoke grenades because their breath created clouds of vapor around their heads in the biting cold.

They hadn't slept in ninety-six hours.

Crushing out a hundred-fifty push-ups, each one so painful he broke out in a sweat, though it was freezing cold and he was wet. Thank God for his combat boots encasing his ankle, because it was swollen, maybe sprained. He didn't want to look. There was blood on his uniform and he had no idea what from. At the last push-up he collapsed to the ground and rolled over, deliberately pissing his pants just to feel a little warmth on his legs.

"*Wright!*" One of the instructors placed a bullhorn over his face and screamed. Dougherty. The recruits called him the Antichrist. "Look over there at that bell! Nice shiny bell! Ring it and this is over! Ring it and I'll personally buy you a fucking room at the fucking Del, where you can sleep for a week on perfumed sheets! What do you say?"

"No, sir!" Max mumbled.

"Can't hear you, Wright!" the bullhorn roared.

"No, *sir!*" Max screamed.

He didn't ring the bell. He'd never ring the bell.

Right now, his movements in the water were slow and he was cold: signs of dangerous exhaustion. He'd known men who had simply passed out in the water from exhaustion and drifted down to their deaths.

Wasn't going to happen.

He passed the two-mile mark, stopping to come up for air, treading water, and to observe the situation. His injured leg had stopped working. He was advancing almost exclusively with his arms, muscles trembling with fatigue.

He reached into the small dinghy for his waterproof bag and pulled out the binocs. They had night vision, and with the press of a button, IR.

He scanned the area carefully, in quadrants, and saw no signs of life around the jetty. If they were expecting trouble, they were expecting it from a boat, not from a lifesaver on steroids.

Another mile to go. But, to be on the safe side, he should make landfall at least fifty meters from the jetty. He saw a little outcropping with bushes where he could hide while getting out of the wet suit and gearing up.

Another mile.

He treaded, waiting.

There was a place inside him. He'd found it during Hell Week. It had been with him on countless missions. He'd lost it when he was blown up and then found it again when he refused to become a cripple.

He needed to find it right now if he had any hope at all of swimming this last mile, when the thought of letting go and drifting down, down, down was so enticing.

That place was still in him, but there was now someone else there, too. Paige.

For the first time in his life, there was another person *inside* him, as much a part of him as his hands and legs. She was indispensable, his heart. The future, any future without her was unthinkable. It would stretch out forever, gray and flat.

This was the first time he'd ever known fear, real fear. A SEAL wasn't afraid to die. SEALs were trained to tackle the worst, most dangerous situations. And no matter how hard the training, how excellent the equipment, shit happens, and it happens a lot in battle. Every warrior in the history of the world knows that.

Every single SEAL he knew had in some way come to terms with his possible imminent death. There had been a few who made it to BUD/S, he suspected, who welcomed death, would go forward smiling to embrace it, because they couldn't even imagine life when they were no longer young and strong.

Luckily, the trainers recognized that and weeded them out. The Teams needed men who weren't afraid to die, not men who wanted to die.

So if death held no terrors, not much else did either.

Except right now, the thought of losing Paige—that terrified him. Losing the light she brought into his life, that sharp mind that kept him on his toes, that vital essence that was purely her. That terrified him.

Paige was It. He'd dated and fucked for more than half his life. He liked women and they liked him, but he recognized now that his head hadn't been in the game—his cock had.

There was a connection there between him and Paige that was bone-deep, blood-deep, a connection that, if severed, would be like severing an artery.

And it was the image of Paige, the memory of her kissing his shoulder before falling asleep, how she'd instinctively slow down to accommodate his leg, how she sleepily smiled at his touch first thing in the morning without opening her eyes . . . those were the things that kept him going when his body quit.

He was going to get out of this alive and he was going to bring Paige home.

And, later, after he'd made love to Paige, oh, about a thousand times just to make sure she was really safe, he knew what he was going to do with his life.

He couldn't be an active SEAL. That was off the cards. But he still had skills, rare skills.

He would never forget the gut-wrenching terror of knowing someone he loved was in hostile hands. That terror would shape the rest of his life. He was going to put his skills at the disposal of those whose loved ones had been kidnapped. He was going to dedicate his life to bringing them home, just as he was going to bring Paige home.

He moved on.

His movements in the water were mechanical, jerky, wasteful, and inefficient. But there it was—a blackness deeper than the blackness of the water right in front of him, rising up out of the ocean.

The island.

A hundred meters, fifty meters, ten meters, five, two . . . his flippered feet touched the rocky bottom and he hauled himself out of the water in the tiny cove he'd detected, hidden from the jetty by bushes. He took two stumbling steps up the rocky shore, pulling the dinghy up behind him, hearing Max leaping out. He couldn't stand up. He fell to his knees, then toppled to one side.

He woke to Max's frantic tongue lapping his face. His non-reflective watch told him he'd only been out for a few minutes. He gritted his teeth against the grinding pain of his leg and managed to stand up. His leg was trembling. It felt like he was walking on ground glass. He was overdoing it. He could lose his leg.

Didn't matter. He could live without his leg. He couldn't live without Paige.

In minutes, he was out of the wet suit and geared-up. The whole time, Max watched him soberly, sitting on his haunches, waiting for the human to get ready.

The instant Max moved toward the jetty, the dog shifted to his side, keeping pace with him, keeping close. Instinctively, the dog understood teammates stayed together.

Max knew how to meld with the night. He moved like a shadow to higher ground, up above the jetty, waiting patiently after each move to see if he'd been spotted. Hurrying and getting caught wouldn't help Paige.

He scanned with the night vision binocs and saw two men

higher up. One smoking, again.

Bad for your health, you scumbag, he thought. *And so's this.*

He went for them.

Even limping badly, it was no contest. They didn't have a chance. They sucked at being security guards, though they did understand the muzzle of a gun to the nape of the neck. There were two guards, but Max was in a team of two, as well. His brave furry friend kept vigil over one of the guards, face-down in the dirt, paws straddling his head, growling low while Max trussed up the first asshole, then the other. Wrist and ankle restraints. Then good old duct tape over the mouth, and he and Max were good to go.

He took their weapons, disassembled the rifles and tossed the pieces into the shrubbery. Took their sidearms, Beretta 92s, and threw them and the magazines into the ocean.

He snapped his fingers and Max heeled. They both moved forward toward the front entrance of the building.

Max kept his nose to the ground. All of a sudden he stopped, snuffled around, then moved forward purposely.

He'd picked up Paige's scent.

Max called the dog back softly. He quivered with impatience but obeyed.

Though his leg was on fire, Max painfully lowered himself behind a bush and observed the door and the guards.

The security system was fairly sophisticated but doable.

If this had been a sanctioned op with air support behind him, Max would have preferred to infiltrate by rappelling down onto the roof from a helicopter, but he didn't have that choice here.

And anyway, Max had been following his nose and had

been headed for the door. Paige had walked through that door a couple of hours ago, and so he and his teammate would, too. He had to follow the dog's lead here.

These guards were a little less Bozo the Clown-ish. They meant business. But then so did he.

He waited, looking for an opening. One of the guards suddenly spoke into a cop-style shoulder mic, swiped a card down the side of the big door, and entered.

Good. So he wouldn't have to blow the door down.

Ten minutes later, the guard came back, put his head next to the other guard's head, and said something. They both laughed.

A wave of coldness swept over him. Were they laughing at the idea of holding a beautiful woman hostage? By his side, Max woofed out a very soft, brief growl.

His partner was growing impatient. Fair enough, so was he.

He was tired of being nice. He shouldered the MP-5, gritting his teeth as he tried to find stability on his bad leg. Goddamn it, wasn't working. It wanted to buckle.

He leaned against the trunk of a big pine and took aim. It had to be a head shot because they had body armor.

Phhht! The asshole with the card dropped as if he were a puppet whose strings had been cut.

Max shifted immediately to the second target and dropped him before he realized what had happened to his partner.

Max limped to the first target and took out the swipe card.

The dog had already bounded to the door, taking an indifferent sniff of the two dead men as he passed. He pointed his muzzle at the door, arrow straight.

Paige was in there somewhere.

There were no biometric data necessary, which was fortunate, though Max was perfectly willing to press a dead man's thumb against a plate or hold a dead man's retina against a scanner. They obviously felt that the water was protection enough.

Wrong.

The building wasn't a commercial building. There was no corporate lobby or even an entrance, really. Just one big corridor that led to other corridors.

This was where Max the dog did his thing.

He leaned down to run his hand over Max's head and said, in a low voice, "Find her, boy. Find Paige."

The dog took off, nose to the ground, and Max followed as fast as he humanly could. Pain jarred him right up to the top of his head every time he put weight on his leg, but he ignored it. There'd be time to take care of his leg later, once he had Paige safely home.

He would never have found her without Max. The dog moved unerringly down corridors it would have taken him hours to check and clear.

It was a labyrinthine building, built for work and not for representation. It was also empty. He encountered no one as he followed Max. At each corner, he'd stop, listen, check with his small angled mirror, then lead with his rifle, but all he encountered was air and a dog turned to him, waiting for him to follow.

There was a drumming need in him now to find Paige, the sense that a clock was ticking down. He hurried as fast as he could, shutting out the grinding pain, the drumbeat of his heart loud in his head. He needed to get to her *now*. Because something was happening *now*.

Finally, Max lifted his muzzle and stopped in front of a door. It was in the middle of a long, wide corridor with very few doors, which meant the rooms were large.

He put his ear to the steel door and heard faint voices. Male voices. Then a softer voice.

Paige!

He tested the door, opening it just enough to slip the mirror in and narrowed his eyes as he watched. The dog stuck his nose into the crack and started wriggling. He could smell his mistress and wanted to go to her.

Max put a hand down to calm the trembling dog.

Max studied the situation in the mirror for long moments, trying to remain dispassionate. Looking at the vectors, figuring the odds, checking line of sight and angles. Because that's what he was trained to do and that's what he did well.

He didn't allow himself to think about what he was seeing.

Paige, bound to a chair, head hanging low. Blood trickling from a cut in her forehead. Paige, with a black eye and swollen jaw. Bruised and battered.

He put his reaction away, tamped it right down, put it in a box and locked it.

Observed.

Three men, two armed. All three with their backs to him.

The unarmed one sitting on a chair to one side of her, one leg crossed over the other, foot casually swinging. The interrogator.

The two armed fucks standing, holding their Berettas loosely by their sides. At that distance, they could never miss. She was tied up. They'd have plenty of time to kill her.

The man in the chair swung his leg idly, got up, walked over, and bent his head close to Paige's—much as a lover would. She moved back in revulsion and he laughed. The sound carried in the big room. He said something else and she spat at him.

It was like a frozen tableau. Nobody moved; it seemed nobody breathed.

The man next to Paige wiped his face, murmured something to her, then clicked his fingers. His voice was suddenly clear and echoed in the room. "Let's end this."

The two armed men raised their gun hands.

Max opened the door wider and lobbed a flashbang right into the geographic center of the triangle formed by the three men and, pulling the dog away with him, flattened his back against the wall next to the door, opened his mouth, and covered his ears.

There was a way to deal with sociopaths, Paige was sure. Unfortunately, she had no idea what it was.

There was no reasoning with Larry—none.

In his money-crazed head, he had the perfect plan for instant riches and the only two people stopping him from raking in amazing wealth were herself and Silvia. To him, once he got rid of these two pesky women, it was going to be smooth sailing. A hole in one.

He was going to kill her. Or, rather, have her killed, as she just couldn't see him pulling the trigger himself. It was there, in his face and in his body language.

Most of it was because he'd convinced himself that she stood in the way of a lifetime of champagne and Rolexes, but a part of it—she understood quite well—was because she had refused him. She'd wounded some deep insecurity in him and she was going to pay.

She'd told him everything she knew, bits and pieces coming out with each blow. The pain was like razor flowers blossoming at odd points of her body. Her jaw, her shoulder, a wrist she suspected was broken when he punched her so hard she fell to the floor again.

The only thing she didn't tell him was about the thumb drive.

If she'd had the slightest hope that he'd let her live, she'd have told him. No question. She ached all over, the pain deep and vicious. Anything to make this stop.

But he wasn't going to stop, and since she was as good as dead, she could leave this earth with the hope that even if they caught Silvia, too, Max could find the thumb drive, figure out what was going on, and go to the cops with the story.

Max wouldn't stop until he found the truth, though in all likelihood they'd never find her body. You can drag rivers and ponds but not the ocean. They'd weight her down, slip her body over the side of that boat, and no one would ever know what had happened to her.

He'd take care of her dog, though.

Oh God. How ironic. She'd never thought to find love, not the wild, pulse-pounding kind. She'd thought maybe someone would come along at some future point. A fellow research scientist, maybe. Some nice guy who didn't turn her off. They'd date for a year or two, then start discussing marriage.

Never, ever, would she have thought love could come in another package. Tall and broad, a warrior. A wounded warrior who woke up every sense she had and made her feel alive down to her fingertips.

And now she was going to lose that love the instant she found it.

"*Tell me!*" Larry said, moving his face close to hers, spittle flying from his mouth. "Goddamn you, you bitch, *talk!*"

He'd asked her a question and she had no idea what it was. Never mind. She didn't even have the strength to raise her head. When she moved it, spikes hammered into her brain and she lost her vision for a second.

She gathered her senses for one last effort and spat at him.

Larry wiped his face and stood up, waving his hand at the two goons behind her. "Let's end this."

They were raising their rifles. Oh God. This was it.

Max, she thought, a solitary tear falling down her battered face. *I love*—

The world exploded.

A flash of blinding light so intense she continued to see it behind closed eyelids, and a noise so loud she heard it through her diaphragm like a punch.

Was she dead? Is this what death was like? So bright and so noisy?

She couldn't think, she could hardly breathe. She opened her eyes, blinked, blinked again. All three men were on the floor, red seeping from their heads. Hands were tugging at her—a knife flashed, a big black one—and she shrank back, hoping it would be quick . . .

But the knife didn't cut into her flesh—it was cutting into the hateful tape binding her. And there was, there was . . . there was *barking*. How could that be?

Suddenly the world righted itself. Max! And Max!

The last strand of tape was cut and she stood up, then fell into Max's arms because her legs wouldn't hold her. His couldn't either. They fell to the floor in a heap and she landed on warm, hard male.

"Oh God," she breathed, her lungs clogged with emotion. "You came for me!"

Max looked awful. Pale and drawn and drained, but smiling as he kissed her. "*We* came for you. Did you doubt we would?"

Her dog was barking, frantically licking her face, front paws on human Max's chest, wiggling and whining with happiness.

"No." the word came out as an explosion of joy. "No, I knew you'd come, both of you."

"Woof!" her Max said.

"Woof!" her other Max said.

"Damn straight," she answered and embraced them both.

One year later
Outside Eugene, Oregon

"Silvia will be here in about an hour," Paige said, flipping her cell phone closed.

Max gave a sly smile. "Cory's really happy. He just bought himself a tie. I never thought I'd see him in a tie, but once he found out she's coming, there was no stopping him."

"A tie and those new titanium-blade legs. He's going to be irresistible." He was, too. Silvia had quietly tried to pry the guest list for their wedding anniversary party out of Paige and hadn't stopped asking until Paige gave in and said Cory'd be there.

"Just as long as he doesn't con me into a race," Max said sourly.

"Because he'll win. And you hate losing." Man, did she know her husband. He'd acquired most of the use of his bad leg back, but no one could keep up with Cory's blades.

"Maybe I'll dare him and if I win he has to join us. That

would be an incentive." Max's company, Search Inc., was very successful. He put together different teams for every search-and-rescue job but Cory was always part of it. Search was growing so quickly, Max wanted a partner and he wanted it to be Cory.

Search wasn't the only thing that was growing, Paige reflected. She placed a hand on her belly and smiled up at her husband.

"Did you get that shipment off?" he asked. "Of . . . things?"

Max still didn't have a complete grasp of what she did and rarely ventured into her propagation lab, a little unsettled by the silence and rows and rows of tiny containers.

"Yes, it's safely gone. And I just got ten new orders." She'd been surprised at the success of her own company, a small propagation laboratory that was growing exponentially. It felt so good to be her own boss and leave the corporate world behind.

She looked out over their home, a restored nineteenth-century homestead that she loved, her gaze taking in her lab and Max's high-tech bunker next to it, where he and his teammates planned their "extractions." It was soul-satisfying work. Last week they'd rescued a four-year-old boy.

The house glowed with candles and everything was ready for the guests, who would start arriving in about an hour.

"It's all good," Max said softly, almost to himself, then smiled down at her. He bent to kiss her, the kiss growing heated, until she pushed at his chest. He lifted his head, dark eyes glowing.

"No," Paige said. "Absolutely not. I just put my makeup on."

Max gave an exaggerated sigh, but didn't stop smiling. "A man can try."

A sharp bark sounded and Paige looked down at her dog. He lifted his muzzle and she could swear he smiled at her.

"Is that a *smile?*" her husband asked.

"I think it is. A smug one."

"Well, he's a father, after all. Puppies will do that."

Paige nestled her head against her husband's shoulder and sighed with happiness. "Well, we'll see how you react to your own puppies." She smiled into his startled face. "We're having twins."

SEALs and Why We Love Them

Dear Reader,

Anyone who has read my books knows I often write about SEALs, simply because I admire them so very much.

I'm a romance writer and so part of what makes my writing heart tick is the appeal of my characters. On that level, any SEAL is off the charts. They are almost caricatures of manliness—brave and strong, with that relentless male focus that can be so effective, and yet can sometimes drive those of us who are married or in a relationship crazy. (I can hear you smiling.)

Their macho is in their minds—not their muscles. I've read lots of books about SEALs and memoirs by SEALs, and what shines through is the incredible intelligence of these men (for they are all men). They are smart in every way there is. They are book-smart *and* street-smart, an unusual and unusually attractive combination. Reading the memoirs, in particular, you find that these men take an often chaotic world and make some kind of sense of it.

The world they operate in is neither orderly nor rational

nor kind, and they must act in ways that are orderly, rational, and, yes, kind. They are bound by rules their enemies do not in any way respect, so we're asking them to go out and fight for us, put their lives on the line for us, and—oh yes, forgot!—please do that with one hand tied behind your back.

I really admire human excellence, particularly the kind that isn't innate, the kind you have to work really hard for. The med student who spends her weekends practicing tying sutures on the bedpost; the pianist who practices those extra hours to be able to put soul—and not just technical perfection—into that Bach sonata; the scientist who runs that test for the ten thousandth time and it turns out successful, when everyone else would have stopped at the thousandth iteration. That is, perhaps, the quintessence of being human.

And, contrary to popular myth, SEALs are human, very human. They are not supermen. Bullets do not bounce off them. They bleed and they hurt and they die. They do what they do in the shadows and they do it for us.

Hats off and my heartfelt gratitude.

Lisa Marie Rice

If you enjoyed *Fatal Heat*, don't miss out on Lisa Marie Rice's exciting *Protectors* series in which three heroes—former Navy SEAL, Delta Force Operator, and Marine Force Recon—walk through fire for the women they love.

Into the Crossfire
A Protectors Novel: Navy SEAL
Available Now

Hotter Than Wildfire
A Protectors Novel: Delta Force
Available Now

Nightfire
A Protectors Novel: Marine Force Recon
Available February 2012

A Protectors Novel: Marine Force Recon

NIGHTFIRE

He would walk through fire for the woman he loves.

Lisa Marie Rice

Author of Hotter Than Wildfire

NIGHTFIRE

Chloe Mason sat in the very elegant waiting room of RBK Security, Inc., which was in a very elegant building in very elegant downtown San Diego.

She'd spent a lot of time in plush, designer surroundings, but she was still impressed with the large room which managed to be both beautiful and designed for comfort and efficiency.

It also had another quality with which she was very familiar. Everything in the room—from the color palette of light earth tones to the lush, healthy plants to the expensive couches and armchairs, the interesting but not shrill modern artwork—was designed to calm and to soothe.

It was still the Christmas season, but the office didn't have the usual loop of nauseatingly familiar carols playing, which many found grating and stressful, particularly if they were in trouble. Rather, the Christmas spirit was honored by soft medieval madrigals playing in the background. Instead of killing a tree, the company had put up a colored light sculpture that was both intriguing and beautiful.

She'd spent all of her childhood and a good deal of her adolescence in and out of very expensive medical clinics, and that mixture of good taste and reassurance was one she knew well.

Even the receptionist was soothing. Chloe had walked into this highly successful office and asked to speak with one of the partners. In American business-dom that just didn't happen. She knew enough of business etiquette to be aware of that.

And yet she hadn't made an appointment. She'd propelled herself here from Boston without even thinking of making one—excited and terrified and hopeful, in equal measure.

So she'd walked over to the elegant "U" design of the reception counter and quietly given her name to the slender, sharply-dressed receptionist with beautiful silver hair cut by someone who knew what he was doing.

The receptionist hadn't blinked at the unexpected request. She simply looked up and asked whether the appointment was urgent.

Urgent? Was it urgent? Maybe, maybe not. Though if Harry Bolt was who she thought he was, it was more than urgent. It was life-shattering.

So she simply nodded, throat too tight to plead her case.

"Okay then," the receptionist had said, tapping on her touch screen. "It's a busy morning for Mr. Bolt, but I'll do what I can." She looked up again, eyes searching Chloe's face. "Would one of the other partners do? Mr. Keillor has a free hour this morning."

Mr. Keillor would be Michael Keillor, former marine, former SWAT officer, current partner. She'd read his bio on the RBK web site and seen his unsmiling photograph. He looked smart and tough and capable, just like all the partners.

If she had security problems, he'd probably be just as good as Harry Bolt.

But her problems didn't have anything to do with security.

She shook her head, hoping the receptionist wouldn't take her inability to speak as discourtesy. And while she was at it, that the receptionist wouldn't notice Chloe's shaking hands.

The receptionist didn't—she simply touched the screen again. "Okay, I can clear you for Mr. Bolt at nine thirty, if you don't mind waiting."

Chloe had waited all her life for this moment. Another half an hour wouldn't make any difference. She managed to choke out a thank-you through her tight throat, and sat down to wait on one of the incredibly comfortable armchairs that dotted the enormous lobby.

So many emotions swirled in her chest that she couldn't feel any single one in particular, just a huge pressure so powerful she could barely breathe. She wanted *so much* for—

And she stopped herself right there. Wanting didn't make things happen. If there was one thing her life had taught her, it was that. She could want so fiercely she thought she would explode, and it wouldn't make any difference at all. It was impossible to understand what really could make a difference. Fate? Perhaps. Randomness? Maybe. Wanting? No.

So she sat back in the extremely comfortable and attractive armchair and . . . disappeared.

It was her trick, learned harshly throughout her childhood. Bad things happened to her when she got noticed. She'd learned very early to sit back and become unnoticeable. She didn't become literally invisible. It's just that she could turn off all the subconscious signals humans sent to each other, so that no one noticed her.

She sat there, unmoving, saying nothing, and observed. Observed the other people waiting for one of the three partners. There were three men in the room, all middle-aged or older, all visibly rich and powerful. Businessmen, who wanted RBK to help them in something or with something. Two were sweating so badly a slightly acrid odor rose above their expensive colognes. The other sat in Male Mode, knees apart, clasped hands between them. He radiated anger and aggression.

Chloe didn't dare look at him. Though she'd perfected the art of blandness, she knew through bitter experience that an angry male took even a chance meeting of eyes as aggression.

She turned her head toward the entrance door so that he couldn't even pretend to think that she was staring at him, and watched as the sliding door swooshed open.

A man walked into the waiting room and all male eyes swiveled to him, watching his progress across the lobby. The three rich-looking men might think that they were alpha males in their own environments, but they weren't. Chloe knew many rich men who thought their money gave them top-dog status anywhere, any time. Often it did, but not always.

This man, striding across the room, was the alpha male. He'd be the alpha male in any grouping—rich man, poor man, didn't make any difference.

He wasn't tall but he was immensely broad—wide shoulders, thick arms, strong neck. A bodybuilder, but without that bodybuilder waddle, because he clearly built onto muscles that were already there. His movements were fast, precise, powerful. The strongest man in the room, hands down. And he'd be the strongest man in the room in most rooms.

Michael Keillor. The K in the RBK. He wouldn't be billionaire-rich but he didn't have to be. He was wealthy, successful, dominant. Enough by any person's measure.

He scanned the lobby as he walked by, eyes dwelling for a moment on her. He didn't break his stride, but Chloe knew he was studying her. She met his eyes, fiercely blue, very intelligent, impersonal and cold. Suddenly he blinked—the coldness vanished and something happened, but she didn't know what.

When he walked in, he'd launched himself across the room as if it were just a way station as he arrowed toward the offices visible behind a glass-plated sliding door, but now he detoured and stopped for a moment at the desk, elbows on the counter, leaning forward to talk to the receptionist.

The woman looked startled, then shot a glance at Chloe.

Her heart gave a painful beat in her chest. He was discussing *her*? Why? Did he have some inkling of why she was here? How could he? No one on earth knew why she was here. Not even old Mr. Pelton, the family lawyer, knew, because she hadn't approached him yet.

Time enough for that if she were successful. Not that Mr. Pelton would ever approve.

No. Her mission here was completely secret.

So why was Michael Keillor discussing her with the receptionist?

It was . . . it was unnatural. Chloe wasn't used to being the focus of anyone's attention. She didn't remember learning the art of passing under everyone's radar. It had always been there and she'd perfected it over the years.

She never dressed outrageously. Her clothes were expensive, but low-key, never too trendy. She was always clean and groomed, but never flashy.

All her life, people had taken one look and simply forgotten her in an instant, walking on by. Chloe didn't want attention. Not out of shyness, but because she was afraid of it. Since she could remember, attention had meant danger. If someone looked at her too closely, her heart began pounding, an instinctive and totally uncontrollable reaction.

Michael Keillor nodded at the receptionist, took another look at her that had her hands sweating, and disappeared through the sliding glass door into the offices at the back of the lobby.

Nine fifteen. The appointment with Harry Bolt was in a quarter of an hour, if he was a punctual man.

Chloe sat back to do what she did best—wait. It seemed almost her entire childhood—what she could remember of it anyway—and adolescence had been spent waiting. Waiting for the scars to heal, waiting for the casts to come off, waiting to recover from the last surgery, waiting for the next one. She was the goddess of waiting. If there were a PhD in waiting, she'd have been awarded one years ago.

She knew exactly how to prepare for a bout of waiting, how to breathe shallowly, slowly, how to distance herself from her body, how to will herself to stillness.

In college, she'd read up on a number of behavioral and mind-control techniques and found that she'd taught them all to herself instinctively, without knowing they existed.

Chloe could outwait anyone. Just sink right down into herself until she needed to come back up.

But right now, it shocked her to realize that none of her techniques worked. Her breath was rapid, almost panting. Her heart trip-hammered in an anxious, uneven rhythm. Her palms were sweaty. There was no way she could will herself back into her well of calm. She kept clutching the manila envelope on her lap over and over again, until the edges were sweat-stained and crumpled. Another sign of huge stress, together with the feeling that there was no oxygen in the room.

She had waited her entire life for this moment, without knowing it. And now that it was here, she wasn't prepared. She would never be prepared. She'd thought and thought about what she would say, but nothing occurred to her. Her mind was empty, hollow and shiny with panic. She didn't even know if she could talk, her mouth was so dry.

Think, Chloe! She told herself sternly. She'd done so many hard things in her life, surely she could do this?

What to say? How to tell if she even should say it? Maybe she'd talk to the man and realize that she'd been insane to rush across the country for this. Maybe—

"Ms. Mason?"

Chloe turned, heart pounding. "Y-yes?" she stammered, sliding forward to the edge of her seat.

The receptionist gave her a kind smile. Considering how upscale this office was, the smile was purely gratuitous. Most receptionists and secretaries in successful big-bucks enterprises were haughty. Certainly Mr. Pelton's was. In all the visits to her lawyer's offices, Chloe had mainly seen Mr. Pelton's secretary's nostrils as she tilted her head up to look down her nose.

"Mr. Bolt is free to see you now. Third door to your right down the corridor." She pointed to the big glass doors next to the reception desk.

Oh God, this is it!

Panic keened in Chloe's head as she slowly rose, hoping her knees would support her. It was a very real fear. Both her knees were complex creations of plastic and steel, and they were as delicate as they were high-tech.

Everyone's eyes followed her as she made her slow way across the lobby, which suddenly felt as huge as the Gobi Desert. The glass door ahead of her was so clean it glowed. How was she supposed to—ah. It swooshed open at some invisible command.

Inside the corridor, the feeling of luxury was even more powerful. The doors were shiny brass, with no door knobs, only built-in flat screens to the right. The rooms must be enormous because it felt like she walked for ages down the gleaming parquet corridor simply to get to the third door on the right.

Here, too, she was met with a wall as blank as her head. She simply stood there, clutching purse and envelope tightly, waiting for the next step. Any thoughts or plans simply vanished from her head. She felt as if she were walking on some kind of uncontrollable path where she could only stumble forward and never turn back.

She stared at the shiny brass door, looking blankly at her reflection, mind emptied of thought for a heartbeat, two. Then there was a whirring sound, a click releasing some invisible mechanism, and this door too slid open.

Chloe stood, frozen, on the threshold. She'd been dreaming of this moment all her life, thinking she was insane because it happened only in her dreams.

When things remained as hopes and dreams you could decide how they turned out. And though not much in her life had turned out well, in her dreams this always had. It had always ended in laughter and joy.

Only in her head, though.

Which was notoriously unstable.

Chloe trembled. Stepping into this room might mean stepping into a new and better life. Or it might forever trap her behind the invisible but oh-so-real wall she'd lived behind all her life.

It felt as if her entire existence were hanging by a thread, by a step.

"Ms. Mason?" a deep voice said and she gasped in air. She'd been holding her breath for almost a minute without realizing it.

Across another vast room, two men were standing, as gentlemen did for ladies. One was Michael Keillor.

She didn't want him there. Her business was exclusively with Harry Bolt, and if her business ended badly, she didn't want anyone else to view her humiliation. But a lifetime of training made her hold her tongue. She didn't even remotely have the courage to ask him to leave the room.

The other man was . . . was Harry Bolt. Chloe eyed him hungrily. Much taller than Michael Keillor and almost, but not quite, as broad. Dark blond hair, light brown eyes. Familiar-looking eyes.

Her heart was slamming against her chest so hard she wondered if they could hear it.

Chloe was used to observing and interpreting body language, but there was absolutely nothing to read here. Both men were utterly still, both were utterly expressionless.

She had no way at all to gauge their feelings. No way to figure out how this would end.

Shaking, with a feeling of doom interlaced with wild hope in her heart, Chloe stepped into the room.

She's scared shitless, Mike thought, glad that he'd horned in on this meeting. This Chloe Mason had specifically asked for Harry Bolt but once Mike had seen her in the lobby, he knew he had to be here, too.

Because this woman was clearly one of the Lost Ones. A woman in trouble, on the run from some violent asshole. And shit, it made him angry all over again that there were monsters in the world who could beat up on women.

RBK mainly dealt with corporate security. In the lobby waiting for RBK's very expensive services, there'd been two CEOs and one head of security for a Fortune 500 company. Mike had read their files, knew what their problems were, and knew how to solve them.

Those three men alone probably represented about a million dollars in business this year for RBK.

Chloe Mason represented nothing, because RBK policy was not to accept money from women on the run. If anything, RBK often provided the women with a little nest egg to see them through that first difficult year.

On average, after the first year, they were safe.

After last night, Mike really, really wanted to make a woman safe. Wanted to help a woman, particularly a woman like this, soft and gentle and completely undeserving of the sick fuck who'd forced her to come to them.

This morning Sam was staying home with Nicole, who had bad morning sickness, so the corporate honchos would be divided between him and Harry. Stuff he and Harry could do with their eyes closed. All three of them had an instinctive understanding of security risks—their entire childhoods had been security risks—and they had been trained very hard and very expensively by Uncle Sam to learn how to deal with risks. It was a question of knowledge and reason. But with their Lost Ones, the trembling and broken women who showed up on their doorstep because RBK was their last chance before falling into the abyss . . . when dealing with them, you used both your head and your heart.

Though the woman in the lobby had asked to see Harry, Mike instinctively knew she was his. He had to be the one to help her.

Not because she was beautiful, though she was. Astoundingly beautiful.

But because she looked so lost, so alone. She was slightly built, with pale skin and pretty, delicate features. A slightly overlarge mouth and huge, light brown, almost golden eyes.

Her clothes were expensive. So were her shoes and purse. Expensive, elegant, discreet. This was a lady of taste and of breeding, and she looked rich.

Didn't matter.

He and his colleagues had seen a lot of everything pass through their doors. Women who'd been beaten up by low-life drug-addict husbands and lovers, sure. But also wives of lawyers and doctors, and even a senator. The rich weren't immune to the joys of beating up on women and children. If anything, they were able to hide it better, and for longer.

The police were also more willing to turn a blind eye.

The rich wives who ended up as one of RBKs Lost Ones sometimes tried going to the police, but their husbands often wielded enormous power and were able to get away with things poorer men went to jail for. The wives of the rich fucks were just as beaten down as their poorer sisters.

This woman, this Chloe Mason, belonged to the rich, there was no mistaking it. And not the new rich, either. She had that understated elegance of someone who didn't need to make a splash, someone for whom good taste came naturally.

From head to toe she was groomed and lovely. But there was something underneath those pretty, expensive designer duds that was a little less lovely.

She moved slowly, exactly like someone who'd been punched hard, in a place covered by clothes. That was a little trick fuckhead men who liked beating up on women and kids learned. Their rages might be uncontrollable, but boy they knew enough to reason it out and punch where it wouldn't show. Last week a banker's wife had come in without a visible scratch on her. Except, of course, for a ruptured spleen that had required eight hours of surgery six months before. It had followed broken ribs and a punch to the liver so hard the liver had sustained damage.

Shitheads knew what they were doing, all right. Even in a fucking rage they knew enough to cover their tracks.

Someone had done something like that to Chloe Mason, who moved so very carefully, as if she would fall down if she didn't watch it.

Oh man. Who could do that to someone like her? Who could do it to any woman or child? But especially to Chloe

Mason, with her soft skin and gentle features and slender build?

He glanced at Harry, expecting him to say something, then glanced again.

What the fuck?

It was like Harry was frozen. He simply stood there, staring at her. Not in a sexual way. Like Sam, Harry loved his wife fiercely and absolutely. He had zero interest in other women since his marriage. But something about this woman riveted his attention. And blocked his tongue, because he wasn't saying anything.

Harry knew as well as Mike that these women needed reassurance. They did not need a male staring at them. Particularly a tall, strong male. That kind of staring came off as aggression and women like Chloe Mason had had a bellyful of that.

Mike elbowed Harry in the ribs, to no effect. Okay, so Harry was out for the count. It was up to him.

"Welcome, Ms. Mason," he said gently to the frightened woman slowly crossing Harry's office. Since Harry wasn't moving, Mike walked around the desk and approached her slowly. No sudden moves, just nice and easy.

She stared up at him and he had to jerk his gaze away because he was staring too, just like his idiot colleague Harry.

Damn, she was . . . she was lovely. The old-fashioned word was exactly right. Nowadays "beautiful" was the technical term used for a woman who worked on herself, got herself some surgical enhancement—who stood out because of the way she was dressed and was made up.

Chloe Mason had a different kind of beauty, made up of perfect skin, delicate features, soft blonde hair, huge golden eyes, and none of that—as far as he could see—enhanced.

So, that's what she'd look like in the morning. After sex.

Mike squelched that thought immediately, ashamed of himself. The last thing this woman needed was a man she looked to for help coming on to her.

She was looking up at him anxiously, then back at Harry, clutching a purse and a big manila envelope, visibly worried because his fuckhead brother had his head up his ass.

Since she looked like she was about to fall down, Mike chanced it and placed a hand under her elbow, as gentlemanly-like as possible, though he wouldn't object to carrying her to the client chair.

No. Not going there, he told himself sternly.

Women who'd been beaten up had antennae that quivered when men were around and in their space, because men in their space was a situation that often ended badly. He didn't want Chloe Mason to have even a moment's anxiety because of him.

So he did the opposite of what he'd done walking, then running, through a bad part of town last night, trolling for trouble. Last night, his entire body had been one hand curled up in the universal *come and get it* sign, two bad-ass drugs in his system—alcohol and testosterone. A potent mix that got lots of men into trouble, true. But Mike had been trained by the best to meet trouble head-on when it came his way. He'd bristled with aggression last night. Aggression was his friend, always had been, had saved his life countless times.

Aggression and sex were his constant companions.

But not now.

Now he needed to dial it all down—reassure this beautiful woman, not frighten her.

"Ms. Mason," he said, nodding his head at the two client chairs in front of Harry's desk. "Please take a seat."

He had a naturally deep voice, slightly rough due to the drinking last night. She stood looking at him, swaying slightly, and for a second he wondered how badly she might be injured. Man, if someone had injured her so badly she could hardly stand, he was going to find out who and quietly, privately, beat the shit out of him.

"Ms. Mason?" he repeated, keeping his voice gentle.

She ducked her head. "Yes, of course. I do apologize. I've—been under some stress lately."

It was the first time he heard her voice. It was as soft as the rest of her, with a musical quality. And a faint British accent.

She was English? Mike dropped his hand when she sat down, then rounded Harry's huge desk again.

She sat perched on the edge of the client chair, one of the most comfortable chairs in the world. By definition, RBK clients were in trouble, and the company wanted them to be comfortable while they talked it out. Chloe Mason didn't look comfortable in that chair, she looked tense as hell.

Silence. Harry was still . . . frozen. Goddamn it. What the fuck was wrong with him?

Mike waited a beat, two. Finally, he broke the silence.

"Ms. Mason. Welcome to RBK Security. My name is Mike Keillor and this is my partner, Harry Bolt." He shot a glance at the silent statue that was his partner and refrained from rolling his eyes. Had Harry gone back to his pattern of sleeplessness with his little daughter? Was he in a walking coma, or what? "I know you asked for an appointment with Mr. Bolt, but we often work on . . . cases together. Before we begin, can we offer you something, a cup of coffee? Or tea?" Thinking of that accent.

"Yes, thank you so much." Her words came out in the rush of loosened tension. "I'd love a cup of tea."

Right call.

Mike waited a second for Harry to move, to wake up, to fucking get with the program. Finally, he pushed the button to Marisa, their receptionist. "Marisa, do you think we could get a cup of tea in here?"

Ordinarily, Mike wouldn't ask Marisa to do refreshment detail, but she was the mother hen of their Lost Ones. Marisa'd been a Lost One herself, and had the scars to prove it. She was a fabulous employee, hard-working and loyal. But for the battered women who made their way to the offices of RBK, Marisa went all out. She pampered them and mothered them and protected them fiercely.

"Yes, sir, right away."

The little interlude relaxed Chloe Mason.

Telling their story was a real ordeal for some women. They were all somehow ashamed, though how they could possibly be ashamed of ending up as someone's punching bag was beyond Mike. This moment out of time was a respite for Chloe. Her breathing pattern evened out. A little color came back to her pretty face.

The door to Harry's office slid open and Marisa walked in with a tray. She'd done them proud. A big teapot, three cups, milk, and home-baked cookies brought in by Sam's wife Nicole, baked by their housekeeper.

"Harry." Mike looked at his brother, barely refraining from

poking him in the side with his elbow again. "You want to pour?"

Harry started slightly, as if he'd actually been asleep and had suddenly woken up. "Sure, ah. Sure." His gaze locked onto the woman's face. "How do you take your tea, Ms. Mason?"

She smiled gently. "Dash of milk, one teaspoon of sugar, thank you."

It was the first time Mike had seen her smile. She was clearly under enormous stress, probably terrified, and yet the smile was genuine, blinding. And transformed her face from quietly lovely to otherworldly beauty. A real looker. She didn't catch your attention the first time or maybe not even the second time, but when she did catch your attention—watch out.

Mike felt a tug somewhere in his chest he didn't ever remember feeling, like someone was pulling at a hook.

They were going to take care of this lovely woman. Keep her safe, take her away from danger.

And then, well—forget about beating the guy up. Mike was going to find the fuckhead who'd hurt her and kill him.

A Protectors Novel

INTO THE
CROSSFIRE

The tough former Navy SEAL swore
he didn't have a heart . . . *until now.*

Lisa Marie Rice

Author of *Dangerous Passion*

Into the Crossfire

Well, well. Look at that.

Sam Reston leaned his shoulder against the wall of the hallway of his office building and simply drank in his fill.

There she was.

His own personal wet dream, standing there in the hallway between his office and hers, desperately scrabbling through a huge, expensive-looking purse.

Everything about her was expensive, classy. Top of the line. Real high maintenance, too. The kind of woman he stepped right around without a second thought because he didn't have the time or the inclination, but shit, with her he'd make an exception.

Any man would.

Nicole Pearce. The most beautiful woman in the world. Certainly the most beautiful woman *he'd* ever seen, hands down.

He remembered every second of the moment he'd first laid eyes on her. Two weeks, three days and thirty minutes ago. But who was counting?

He'd been under cover, infiltrating a gang of smugglers and thieves working the docks. His client, a big shipping company, had found it impossible to get a handle on the losses incurred during transhipment at the docks, which last year had totaled almost $10 million.

The police had gotten nowhere and the company suspected that someone somewhere was being bought off. Sam hoped it wasn't in the police department. His brother Mike was a SWAT officer with the San Diego PD and incredibly proud of it.

Someone had definitely dropped the ball, though. So the ship owner had decided to go private.

Smart move.

For a hell of a lot of money, Sam had gone under cover, working the night shift as a stevedore, spreading word around that he wasn't averse to some under-the-table money. He'd been contacted, and had quickly made his way up the hierarchy of the Bucinski gang, finally rising to the point where they had included him on two major hauls. He'd been wired to the teeth and had about a hundred photographs nailing gang members, their scumbag boss, and three corrupt Port Authority employees.

The fuckheads had not just been stealing cargo, they were involved in sex trafficking, too, bringing in kidnapped young girls hidden in the holds of legitimate ships, the owners of the ships entirely unaware of their human cargo.

The whole gang was going down. The shitheads deserved

the needle but wouldn't get it. Each of them would, however, spend the next twenty to thirty being some gangbanger's newest girlfriend, which might even be better.

So Sam had looked like a scumbag the day he first saw her. *Being* a scumbag had been his job for the previous two weeks.

When San Reston did something, he did it well.

Going under cover wasn't like in the movies. You ate, dressed, acted and even smelled the part. While under cover, he rarely washed or shaved, and wore the same clothes for days at a time. He knew he smelled ripe and looked dangerous. Well, hell. He *was* dangerous—he was murderous with rage at the thought of fuckheads willing to rape little girls spending even one day out of jail.

He'd been up thirty-six hours straight and was just coming into the office after another all-nighter to shower, change and grab a few z's on his very comfortable office couch when he'd seen her.

Actually, he smelled her before he saw her. The elevator pinged, the doors opened and some floral . . . thing that traveled into men's heads through the nasal passageways and fucked with their brains reached out and walloped him.

He saw her a second later and froze. Simply froze. Later, when he'd untangled his head from his ass, he'd been amazed. He'd been a SEAL until his eardrum blew, and he'd been a damned good one.

SEAL training beats surprise right out of a man. You have to have good, solid nerves just to think of trying out for BUD/S. If you were the easily surprised type, you were weeded out fast.

Nothing took him by surprise, ever.

Except Nicole Pearce.

Sam had known that the tiny studio office across the hall had been rented out. The building's manager had told him. To a translation agency—though Sam had no fucking idea what that could be—run by one Nicole Pearce.

He hadn't thought more about it.

That particular morning he was more exhausted, filthy and pissed off than usual. He smelled, too, of sweat and beer. He was in a shitty mood, ready to cut the job short simply to get the top guys into the slammer fast. But he knew better. With the evidence he was getting, the entire operation would go down and that was worth a few extra days or weeks living with slime.

A second after that amazing, womanly smell chock-full of pheromones went straight to his dick, he saw her, and his entire body seized up. He was unable to move, unable to breathe, for a second or two.

Midnight black, glossy shoulder-length hair, enormous, uptilted eyes the exact color of the cobalt glass sculpture he'd turned down as too expensive for his office, eyes with lashes so long and thick they could stir up a breeze, slightly overlarge mouth with that Angelina Jolie dent in the bottom lip, perfect straight little nose, creamy skin.

Fuck-me shoes.

Incredible hourglass figure poured into a demure blue suit that exactly matched the color of her eyes and hugged curves guaranteed to make any male within a one-mile radius salivate.

She sure had the two moving guys salivating, as she directed them carrying in a heavy teak desk and a tiny antique sofa. They were doing her bidding like two puppy dogs hoping for a bone.

She turned to look at him directly, at the *ping* of the elevator, and Christ, all he could do was stare at the dazzler with the deep blue eyes.

Eyes that watched him warily.

Sam was exhausted, but a man would have to be dead not to have all his hormones wake up at the sight of the most beautiful woman on earth. And, hell, his hormones weren't the only thing to wake up.

Instant boner, right there in the upscale hallway of the very expensive building he'd chosen as headquarters of his new company.

Shit.

Thank God he had on his tightest jeans because she was already looking alarmed at the sight of him. Who could blame her? He'd put a lot of care into looking like a scumbag, walking like a scumbag, thinking like a scumbag, even smelling like one.

And he was enraged down to the bone at the sex trafficking he'd discovered. That was something that was hard to switch off.

A woman like this would have antenna way out there where men were concerned. She'd be able to read men like other women read fashion magazines. It was a fact of her life. She was stunning, with the kind of natural good looks that would carry her through from childhood to old age as a beauty. So she'd grown up with the background buzz of hot male attention and she'd have learned to filter out the bad ones, the dangerous ones pretty quick.

He wasn't bad but he *was* dangerous and he carried that with him, like a shroud. He'd had a brutal childhood and had learned street fighting before he could read. By adulthood, he was really good with his fists, with a knife, hell—with a rock. Uncle Sam had taken what he was by nature, refined it, armed him up and spent over a million dollars turning him into a killing machine.

He'd made his living as a soldier leading hard men, and now as a civilian he made his living being tougher than most.

He'd come straight into the office after working the night shift on the docks, then sharing a beer with the man who'd recruited him for Bucinski, Kyle Connelly. Sam had nursed one beer to Connelly's ten, and laughed while the pusbag told him about the perks of the job. Extra money, all the drugs you could snort or shoot up and sex. Sam had had to listen while Connelly bragged about handcuffing a twelve-year-old Vietnamese girl to a steel post and raping her. Sam had even had to commiserate with the fucker, whining because he'd been sore afterward, after popping the girl's cherry.

Listening to this, laughing, slapping him on the back in sympathy, had been one of the hardest things he'd ever had to do in his hard life. His hands had literally itched to draw out the garrote wire in his belt and rip the fucker's head right off.

So he'd been fighting mad when the doors had opened and—*whoa*. The world's most beautiful woman, right there in front of him.

He'd actually had to rub his eyes, sure that what was right before him had to be some kind of vision, maybe some kind of compensation for the horrible night.

Her eyes had widened when she'd seen him. He knew what she was seeing—a very large, very strong, hugely pissed-off man, dressed like a bum and smelling like one, too.

Well, he couldn't shave, wash and change his clothes right

then and there and there was nothing he could do to kill those deadly pissed-off vibes so he'd merely walked down the corridor and entered his office.

Her huge cobalt blue eyes had followed him warily every step of the way. She'd actually stepped back as he approached, which pissed him off even more. Goddamn it, the last thing he'd ever do was hurt a woman.

Though, in fairness, she couldn't possibly know that. Probably every cell in her single urban female body was screaming *danger*. He knew she was single because though he saw she had some fancy rings on those pretty hands of hers, none of them were on her left-hand ring finger.

She absolutely had to be single because Sam couldn't even remotely imagine a man married or even engaged to a looker like that who wouldn't put a rock the size of her head on her finger, to warn other men off her. And what husband or fiancé wouldn't be around to help his woman move into her new office?

She couldn't know that his rage wasn't in any way directed at her, of course, but at the system. He wanted to nail the gang *right now* and send them all into the slammer five minutes later, special treatment reserved for one Kyle Connelly, child rapist.

But what you want and what you can have are very different things. No one knew that more than he did. So he'd had to stay under cover, sick at heart, wondering if some other little girls were being raped while he put together enough evidence to put the fuckers away. And to do that he had to stay in Scumland for another couple of weeks.

So every time Nicole Pearce saw him, he'd been tired and grim and dirty, inside and out. Dealing with the scum of the earth was filthy work.

He knew that while he was on this mission, there was no room for anything else, certainly not something as beautiful as Nicole Pearce, so he'd waited.

But all that was now behind him and life had just handed him a big fat present all wrapped up in a fancy bow, to thank him for his patience.

Nicole Pearce, outside her office, looking as beautiful as ever, even with a ferocious scowl on her face, rifling through her bag and jacket pockets, looking for her keys.

The keys to the flimsiest piece-of-shit lock he'd ever seen. When he'd signed the lease on his office, he'd been happy with the space and the location and—though he ordinarily didn't give a shit about his surroundings—the classiness of the building. It was the kind of building that made clients relax, which was crazy to him. What the fuck difference did mellow earth tones and fancy designer junk make?

But to most people it made a difference. A huge one. He'd noticed that. Noticed tense clients start unwinding after entering the building, with its liveried doorman, elegant brass and teak fittings, slate floors, expensive floral arrangements scattered around.

The building supervisor had given him the name of some office designer, who'd come in, taken measurements of the huge space he'd rented and come back a week later and outfitted the office so it looked like a spaceship. A designer spaceship, sleek and comfortable. It all cost a fortune but it was worth it, to see his clients' faces as they walked in.

Anyone who came to Reston Security by definition needed relaxing, and it was good that his office did the trick because

Sam wasn't good at putting people at ease. He had no charm and no small talk in him.

When Sam came across a problem, he wanted it solved yesterday. He became an arrow shooting straight at a solution.

That attitude had worked real well for him in the Teams, where problems and possible solutions were clearly stated and no one's goddamned feelings ever came into anything.

Civilian life had been a bitch, as Sam found himself tussling with clients who were afraid to say what they wanted, who kept intel from him, who had hidden agendas. Christ.

So the upscale, soothing premises had come in real handy.

Not to mention Nicole Pearce, right across the hallway from him, right now scrabbling for keys that weren't there.

Well, he could do something about that. For a price.

"Need some help?" he asked, and suppressed a smile when she nearly jumped right out of that gorgeous skin of hers.

"Need some help?" the scary lowlife who worked for the security company across the hallway asked.

Nicole Pearce's head whipped around, heart kicking up into a hard panicky beat in her chest. Oh God, there he was, long and broad and dark and grim. And frightening as hell.

He hadn't been there a minute ago. Everyone on her floor came in well before her company's opening time of 9 A.M., so she had been sure she was alone as she scrabbled in her purse, quietly freaking out.

How could such a large man move so quietly? Granted, her

head was completely taken up with the tragedy of *no key*, but still. He was huge. Surely he'd have to have made some noise?

Come to think of it, the times she'd seen him coming and going from what she assumed was his workplace across the hall, he'd been utterly silent. Frightening.

She looked at him warily, hands still in her large purse that often doubled as a briefcase.

He was standing with arms crossed, leaning back against the wall, looking completely out of place in the elegant hallway. Tall, immensely broad-shouldered, grim and unsmiling. Just perfect if Central Casting had sent out an urgent call. *One thug. Huge. Intimidating. Report to set.*

But it hadn't. Central Casting populated the Morrison Building in downtown San Diego with perfectly nice, perfectly tame office workers, some a little flamboyant if they were in the advertising business, but otherwise harmless.

Lowlife had absolutely no business here, staring at her out of dark, steady eyes, gaze still and unwavering, completely out of place in the context of the cream and teal accents, the expensive Murano wall sconces and the faux Louis XV Philippe Starck Plexiglas console with the very real calla lilies in the Steuben vase.

She'd chosen to pay premium rent for a tiny office in the upscale building near Petco precisely because its classy, elegant design had appealed to her and because, well, it shrieked success so loudly she hoped no one could hear the crackling sound of financial distress underlying her new company.

Everyone in the building bustled in and out in morning and evening waves, well dressed, well groomed and busy busy busy. Even after the stock market crash, they all made an effort to look sleek and prosperous and successful, which was why Low-life was so out of place.

The rent took a big chunk out of the earnings of her brand-new company, and her office was the size of a thimble, but she loved it. She'd signed the lease half an hour after the realtor had shown it to her.

That was, of course, before Lowlife started haunting the halls. Every time she turned around, it seemed, he was there. Enormous, dressed like a biker. Or how she imagined a biker would dress—what would she know? Bikers had been scarce growing up in consulates and embassies around the world.

He had a uniform of torn, filthy jeans, a formerly black tee shirt washed so many times it was a dirty gray, and at times a black leather bomber jacket.

Overlong black hair and a heavy, scruffy black beard, nothing at all like the chic designer stubble sported by the guys working at the ad agency two doors down. No, this was a man with a heavy beard who didn't shave for weeks at a time.

But beyond not following the yuppie dress and grooming code, Lowlife was different in other ways from all the other people in the building.

She would never forget her first sight of him in the elevator, leaning one-armed against the wall, head down, looking like a warrior who had just come in from battle.

Only there was no war going on in downtown San Diego that she knew of. He'd disappeared into the office across the hall, passing some pretty fancy security, so she'd imagined he worked there.

As an enforcer?

She'd been aware of his scrutiny as she entered and exited

her office. He never overtly stared, but she could feel his attention on her like a spotlight.

Now, however, God help her, he was definitely staring, arms crossed over that absurdly broad chest, unsmiling, gaze fierce and unwavering.

"Need some help?" he asked again. His voice matched his physique. Low, so deep it set up vibrations in her diaphragm.

Then again, maybe the vibrations were panic.

No key.

This definitely wasn't happening. Not on top of the Ride from Hell in to work. Of all the days to lock herself out . . .

"No, I'm on it." Nicole bared her teeth in what she hoped he'd take as a smile, because she so *wasn't* on it.

What she didn't have—and what she so very desperately needed—was her office key. The office key on her Hermès silver key fob that had been a birthday present from her father, back in the days when he could work and walk on his own. The set of keys that was always, always, in the front pocket of her purse, except . . . when it wasn't.

Like now.

Nicole Pearce contemplated beating her head against the door to her office, but much as she'd like to, she couldn't. Not under Lowlife's dark, intense gaze. She'd save that for when he finally left.

He watched as she once more checked her linen jacket pockets, first one, then the other, then her purse, over and over again, in a little trifecta routine from hell.

Nothing.

It was horrible having someone see her panic and distress. Life had taken so much from her lately. One of the few things left to her was her dignity, and that was now circling the drain, fast.

She tried to stop herself from shaking. This was the kind of building where you keep up appearances and you never lose your cool, ever. Otherwise they'd raise the rent.

It was so awful, fumbling desperately in her purse, sweat beading her face though the building's powerful air conditioners kept the temperature at a constant 62 degrees. She could feel sweat trickling down her back and had to stop, close her eyes for a second and regain control. Breathe deeply, in and out.

Maybe Lowlife would disappear if she just kept her eyes closed long enough. Realize that she deeply, *deeply* wanted him gone. Do the gentlemanly thing and just go.

No such luck.

When she opened her eyes again, the man was still there. Dark and tough, a foot from the console she wanted to use.

She looked at the slate floor and the transparent console and gritted her teeth.

Of the two horrible choices, getting close to him to dump the contents of her purse on the console was marginally more dignified than simply squatting and dumping everything in her purse on the floor.

Approaching him warily—she was pretty sure he wasn't dangerous, and that he wouldn't attack her in broad daylight in a public building, but he was so very *big* and looked so incredibly *hard*—she reached the pretty console, shifted the vase of lilies the super had changed just yesterday, opened her purse wide and simply upended it over the transparent surface.

The clatter was deafening in the silent corridor.

She had her home keys, car keys, a removable hard disk, a

silver business card case, a cell phone, four pens, a flash drive—all of which made a clatter. And her leather bag of cosmetics, paperback book, checkbook, notepad, address book, credit-card holder, all of which made a mess.

In a cold sweat of panic, Nicole pushed her way through the objects on the console, checking carefully, over and over again, reciting each object under her breath like a mantra. Everything that should be there was there.

Except for her office key.

What a disaster. Construction on Robinson had forced her into a long detour, which was why she was opening the office at 9:15 instead of 9. At 9:30, she had a vital videoconference with a very important potential client in New York and her two best Russian translators, to negotiate a big job. A huge job. A job that could represent more than 20 percent of her income next year. A job she desperately needed.

Her father's medical bills kept rising, with no end in sight. She'd just added a night nurse for weeknights and it was $2,000 a month. A new round of radiotherapy might be necessary, Dr. Harrison had said last week. Another $10,000. It was all money she didn't have and had to earn. Fast.

If the conference call went well, she might be able to keep ahead of her money problems, for a while at least.

There was absolutely no time to cross all of downtown to go back home and get the keys. Not to mention the fact that she would upset her father, who was so ill. He'd be worried, be unsettled all day. Sleep badly that night. She absolutely didn't want to upset him.

Nicholas Pearce had a limited number of days to his life and Nicole was determined that they be as peaceful as possible.

She simply couldn't go back home. And she simply couldn't afford to miss this meeting. Her translation business, Wordsmith, was too new to be able to risk passing up this client— manager of one of the largest hedge funds in New York, looking to invest in Siberian gas futures and the Russian bond market, and needing translations of the technical data sheets and market analyses.

Sweat trickled down her back. She made a fist out of her trembling hand and beat it gently on the console, wanting to simply close her eyes in despair.

This was *not* happening.

"I can open your door for you." She jolted again at the words spoken in that incredibly low, deep voice. Heavens, she'd forgotten about Lowlife in her misery. His dark eyes were watching her carefully. "But it'll cost you."

This was not a good economic moment for her, but right now she'd be willing to pay anything to get into her office. Snatching up her checkbook from the clear surface of the console, she turned to him. He watched her with no expression on his face at all. She had no reason to think he was a decent sort of guy, but she could hope he wouldn't use her obvious desperation to make a killing.

Please, she prayed to the goddess of desperate women.

"Okay, name your price," she said, flipping back the cover, womanfully refraining from wincing when she saw her balance. God, please let him not ask the earth, because her checking account would go straight into the red. She steadied her hand. *Don't let him see you tremble.*

She looked up at him, pen hovering over her checkbook. "How much?"

"Have dinner with me."

She'd actually started writing, then froze. "I—I beg your pardon?" She stared for a second at the blank check where she'd started writing *dinner with Lowlife* on the line with the amount.

"Have dinner with me," he repeated. Okay, so it hadn't been an auditory hallucination.

Her mouth opened and absolutely nothing came out.

Have dinner with him? She didn't know him, knew nothing about him except for the fact that he looked . . . rough. Instinctively, she stepped back.

He was watching her carefully, and nodded sharply, as if she'd said something he agreed with. "You don't know me and you're right to be cautious. So let's start with the basics." He held out a huge, callused, suntanned and none-too-clean hand. "Sam Reston, at your service."

Sam Reston? Sam *Reston?*

Nicole couldn't help it. Her eyes flicked to the big shiny brass plaque, right next to the door across the hall, bearing the name of what she understood to be the most successful company in the building. RESTON SECURITY. He followed her gaze and waited until she looked back at him.

Maybe he was the company's owner's black-sheep cousin. Or brother. Or something.

It had to be asked. "Are you, um, a relative of Mr. Reston?"

He shook his head slowly, dark eyes never leaving hers. "Company belongs to me."

Oh. Wow. How embarrassing.

He was standing there, hand still out. Nicole's parents had drummed manners into her. She'd shaken hands with tyrants and dictators and suspected terrorists in embassies all over the world. It was literally impossible for her not to put her hand in his.

She did it gingerly, and his hand just swallowed hers up. The skin of his palm was very warm, callused and tough. For a moment she was frightened that he might be one of those men who had to prove his manliness by the strength of his handshake. This man's hand could crush hers without difficulty and she made her living at the keyboard.

To her everlasting relief, he merely squeezed gently for three seconds then released her hand.

"N-Nice to meet you," she stammered, because really, what else could she say? "Um—" And she so desperately needed to get into her office. *Now.* "My name is Nicole Pearce."

"Yes, I know, Ms. Pearce." He bent his head formally. His eyes were very dark and—she now realized—very intelligent. "So—as to my price, let's see if I can convince you I'm not a security risk."

He pulled out a slim, hugely expensive cell phone. One Nicole had coveted madly, both for its function and style, but had decided against as being simply way out of her current financial league. He pressed two buttons—whoever he was calling was on speed dial—and waited. She could hear the phone ringing, then a deep male voice answering, "This better be good."

"I've got a lady here I want to ask out for dinner but she doesn't know me and she's not too sure of my good character, Hector, so I called you for an endorsement. Show your face and talk to the lady. Her name's Nicole. Nicole Pearce." He waited a beat. "And say good things."

Nicole accepted the cell phone gingerly. The video display showed the darkly handsome face of San Diego's brand-new mayor, Hector Villarreal, dressed in a bright orange golf shirt, holding a golf club over his shoulder, out on the links, eyes crinkling against the bright sunlight. "Hello, Ms. Pearce." The deep voice sounded cheerful.

She cleared her voice and tried not to sound wary. "Mr. Mayor."

"So." He was smiling, eyebrows high. "You want to go out to dinner with Sam Reston? You *sure* you want to?" There was humor in the faintly-accented voice.

"Well, actually, uh—"

But it was no use talking to a politician, they talked right over you.

"Don't worry about it. Sam's a great guy, he'll treat you right, no question. But I really do need to warn you of something, Ms. Pearce, and it's serious."

Her heart thudded and she looked up into Sam Reston's hard, impassive face. He could hear perfectly, since Mayor Villarreal was talking at the top of his voice.

"Yes, Mr. Mayor?"

"Don't ever play poker with him. Man's a *shark*." A loud guffaw and the connection was broken.

Nicole slowly slid the phone closed and looked up at Sam Reston. He was standing utterly still; the only thing moving was that enormous chest as he breathed quietly. He had the extreme good taste not to look smug or self-satisfied. There was no expression at all on that hard, dark, bearded face. He simply watched her to see what she would do.

She held out the phone by one end and he took it by the

other. For a moment they were connected by five inches of warm plastic, then Nicole dropped her hand.

They looked at each other, Nicole frozen to the spot, Lowlife—no, Sam Reston—as still as a dark marble statue. There was no sound, absolutely nothing. The building could have been deserted, there weren't even the normal sounds of air-conditioning or the elevators swooshing up and down.

Everything was still, in suspended animation.

Nicole finally took a deep breath.

Ooooo-kay.

Well, it looked like Lowlife—Sam Reston—wasn't a serial killer or a drug dealer. Actually, he, um, was the owner of a company she knew to be very successful. The success of Reston Security constituted a significant portion of the gossip machine that was alive and well in the Morrison Building. Reston Security was certainly much more successful than Wordsmith, which was clinging to life by the occasional IV line of new clients.

If the extremely dangerous-looking, seriously scruffy man in front of her, watching her quietly, was Sam Reston of Reston Security, then surely she could do this.

A deal was a deal. If he could somehow open her door and allow her to make her videoconference call, she would owe him far more than could be repaid by a couple of hours spent consuming a meal.

He was watching her quietly, and standing oh-so still.

9:23. She took a deep breath. "Okay, you have a dinner date, for an evening of your choosing." She gestured behind her. "But you're going to have to open my door, Mr. Reston, right now. I have a very important business call coming in at 9:30 sharp, and if I don't make that call, then our deal is off."

He dipped his head gravely. "Fair enough. And the name is Sam."

"Nicole." Nicole gritted her teeth, glancing at the big clock at the end of the corridor and wincing. However Sam Reston was going to get her into her office, he'd have to do it in the next six minutes or she was toast. "I wonder . . . is there a building super with a master key?"

"No." He shook his head. "So—we have the deal?"

"Um, yes. We do." Nicole barely refrained from tapping her toe.

"You'll go out to dinner with me tonight?" he pressed. At her look, he shrugged broad shoulders. "Ever since I left the Navy and became a businessman, I've learned to nail agreements down."

Actually, he looked like the kind of man who would enforce deals at the end of a gun. But she'd promised.

"As a new businesswoman myself, I've learned to keep my word. So, yes, I accept your invitation. Now, please open my door. And if you kick it open, I'll expect you to pay damages."

"Of course," he murmured.

Nicole shot a glance at her watch. Damn. It had taken her several days to set up this conference call. The client was a Wall Street "Master of the Universe," almost impossible to pin down to an appointment.

The "Master" in question was an anal retentive and when he said a 9:30 conference call, it would be 9:30 to the second, and she knew that he'd never call again if she wasn't on the line. In a harsh, nasal New Yawk accent, the words spilling out almost more quickly than she could understand them, he'd told her he couldn't have anyone wasting his time because his time was worth at least a thousand dollars a minute.

The message couldn't have been clearer. *Be at the end of the line at 9:30 or else.*

Nicole worked with two retired professors of economics, one of whom had been born in Russia and had come to the States as a teenager, and another who had studied in Moscow for ten years. They would be perfect for the big, long-term translation job and she had every intention of asking the Master of the Universe top prices. Her commission off the deal would go a long way toward paying for the night nurse.

Four minutes to go. She was going to lose this appointment, and probably the client. So much for . . .

She looked up from her wrist and blinked.

Her door was wide open, her tiny, pretty office beckoning beyond it.

She turned her stunned gaze to Sam Reston, who was straightening and moving away from her door. "How did you *do* that? Did you just pick the lock?" Surely picking a lock required some kind of effort? Some time? In the movies, the thief jiggled at the lock forever.

He wasn't looking smug or even proud of himself. In fact, he was scowling. "You haven't improved on the building security at all," he said, his deep voice making it an accusation.

"Um, no." Nicole felt like she'd fallen into a rabbit hole. The real-estate agent had stressed the excellent building security and had dwelled lovingly on the quality of the office locks. "Was I supposed to?"

"Well, sure. When it's as crappy as this." His scowl deepened as he pocketed something. Though she'd love to see if it was a lockpick, she didn't have time to waste.

Another glance at her watch and she hurried into her office. She was just barely going to make the videoconference.

She had less than two minutes to spare.

"Thank you, Mr. Reston. So I guess—"

"Sam."

"Sam." She gritted her teeth. A minute and a half left. "Tell me where to meet you and when."

His scowl grew deeper. "Absolutely not. I'll pick you up at your house."

There wasn't time to argue, not even time to roll her eyes. "Okay. Shall we say seven? I live on Mulberry Street. Three forty-six Mulberry Street. Is that okay?"

"Fine. I'll be there at seven to pick you up." A muscle in his jaw rippled, though the words were low and quiet.

Did he live far away? Well, if he had to drive across town, he'd asked for it. She'd been willing to meet him at the restaurant.

He turned away, she closed the door and the phone rang.

Nicole leaped to pick it up, heard the Master's nasal tones. She'd made it! The price had been high, but she'd made it.

A Protectors Novel: Delta Force

HOTTER THAN
WILDFIRE

This former Delta operator would die
to protect the woman who saved his life.

Lisa Marie Rice

Author of *Into the Crossfire*

HOTTER THAN WILDFIRE

San Diego

Ellen Palmer checked the address on the small brass plaque outside an elegant, super-modern building in downtown San Diego against the scrawled words torn off a napkin and verified that they were the same.

She didn't need to do that. She had a near-photographic memory, and if a number was involved, she never forgot it, ever.

Morrison Building, 1147 Birch Street.

Yes, that was it.

Ellen recognized what she was doing. She was stalling, which was unlike her. She was alive because she'd been able to take decisions fast and act on them immediately. She'd have been six feet under if she hadn't acted fast. Stalling was unlike her.

But she was so damned *tired*. Tired of running, tired of lying, tired of keeping her head down, in the most literal sense of the term. Security cameras were everywhere these days and her enemy had a powerful face recognition program. For the past year, she'd rarely presented her naked face in public in daylight.

Even now, when she was betting her life on the fact that she was moving toward safety, she had on huge sunglasses and her now-long hair was drawn forward around her face. She needed to buy a big straw hat.

There were two security cameras on the lintel of the twelve-foot street door of the Morrison Building, but Ellen kept her head down as she entered, walked across the huge glass and marble lobby and rode up in the elevator to the ninth floor. Remaining anonymous in the elevator was hard. The four walls were polished bronze that reflected as well as mirrors to the small security camera in the corner.

The door to RBK Security was guarded by two security cameras, and you were either buzzed in or you dealt with a topflight security panel located on the right-hand side, because the door had no doorknob.

She lowered her head even more as a whirring sound came from above her head. Good God, their cameras were motorized!

Well, it *was* a security company, and she'd been assured they were really good.

They'd better be, because otherwise she was dead.

She rang the bell. There was a click and the door slid silently open. Ellen walked in gingerly, heart starting to pound.

Was this a good idea? Because if it wasn't, if she was putting herself into the wrong hands, there was no turning back, and she'd pay the ultimate price.

The lobby was wonderful—luxurious yet comfortable, with huge, thriving plants, soft classical music in the background, the faint smell of lemon polish, deep, plush armchairs. A secretary sat behind a U-shaped counter. She smiled in welcome.

"Are you Ms. Charles? Mr. Reston will be in shortly. Please have a seat."

For a second, Ellen didn't respond, thinking the receptionist was talking to someone else. But there wasn't anyone else around.

She closed her eyes in dismay. Of course.

She'd booked the appointment under the name Nora Charles, which was stupid. Any film buff would recognize it as a fake name, but she'd been so desperate when she'd called and she'd just sat through a triple feature of *The Thin Man, After the Thin Man* and *Shadow of the Thin Man* last night in San Francisco, waiting for the first bus to San Diego. An all-nighter at the cinema was the only thing she could think of to stay off the streets.

She'd started the journey the day before yesterday in Seattle and hadn't slept more than an hour or two in three days.

But exhaustion was no excuse.

Forgetting her cover name was terrifyingly dangerous. She was alive because she was always alert, always. Forgetting her cover name for just a second was inviting death. And if there was one thing the past year had taught her, it was that she didn't want to die. She wanted—desperately—to live.

Nora Charles was her fifth cover name in twelve months. *Forget all the others and concentrate on this one,* she told herself.

She was mentally putting together a little fake bio for Nora, just to give Nora a little heft in her head, when the receptionist suddenly said, "Yessir, I will."

Ellen really was exhausted, because she couldn't figure out

who the receptionist was talking to. There was no one else in the lobby and she wasn't talking into a phone. Then she saw the very neat, very small and very expensive headset attached to one ear and understood.

Wow. She should have noticed it.

This was truly dangerous. Her exhaustion was catching up with her. She felt stupid with fatigue. Stupid people died, very badly. Particularly ones with Gerald Montez and his army after them.

"Ms. Charles?"

Ellen looked up. "Yes?"

"Mr. Reston has been delayed. But Mr. Bolt is free. They are both partners in the company."

"How—how long will Mr. Reston be delayed?"

"He doesn't know." The receptionist had a kindly look, unusual in such upscale surroundings. Usually an employee in such a swank, obviously successful company was snooty and remote. This woman looked gentle. As if she somehow understood. "It might be a long time. Mr. Bolt is very good, too."

Oh, God. Kerry, the woman who'd told her about RBK Security, had dealt with Sam Reston, who'd saved her life. She had no idea what this Mr. Bolt was like. Maybe Sam Reston worked on the down low to rescue women in danger and this Bolt didn't know anything about it. What then?

Ellen closed her eyes for just a second, wishing she could either rewind her life to a year ago or fast forward to a year in the future, when either she'd be settled in a new life or she'd be dead. Because if she didn't do something, *now*, she was surely headed toward a slow and painful death.

Gerald Montez didn't forgive.

But she kept having to make these split-second decisions, with no training for them, no way to judge whether she was making the right choice or throwing her life away.

The lion or the lady, every time, every day.

And now toss exhaustion and sleeplessness into the mix. How to choose?

She looked the receptionist in the eyes. Ellen was a good judge of character, and now she had to trust her instincts. The receptionist looked back at her calmly, seemingly undisturbed that the lunatic lady, who looked as if she hadn't slept in three days because she hadn't, was staring her in the face, taking minutes for a decision that shouldn't take a second.

Except—like all her decisions this past year—her life hung in the balance.

The receptionist stayed calm, eyes kind. Maybe she was used to desperate people. Maybe the desperate were tossed up on this doorstep daily.

"Okay," Ellen finally said, clutching her hands. *Please let this be the right choice.* She sent the prayer up to whoever was up there, who'd been noticeably absent lately. "I'll see Mr. Bolt. Thank you."

The receptionist nodded. "The second door to your right. Mr. Bolt's name is on the door. He's waiting for you."

Ellen nodded and slowly made her way to the big corridor on the right. As she passed in front of the desk, the receptionist looked up and Ellen saw understanding in her eyes.

"It will be okay," the receptionist said softly. "Don't worry. Mr. Bolt will make it okay."

No, it wouldn't be okay. It would never be okay again.

Harry sat at his desk, trying to clear his mind of his last client, London Harriman, heiress to a real estate empire. She wanted him to stop publication of a sex tape by a tabloid website.

She didn't mind that the sex tape was going to be put online, mind you. Oh no. She'd recorded it specifically in order to release it and she'd assured him that it had been shot "professionally." No, what had got her panties—or lack of panties—in a twist was that she wouldn't be in control of the timing or the release venue.

She wanted him to stop the gossip website from putting it up. She'd handed him a copy with a coy smile, saying she wanted him to watch it. So he'd understand.

London had come on to him, real heavy, but then Harry imagined that London came on to anything with a penis, particularly if that man could even marginally help her in her goal of becoming the Socialite Sex Goddess of the World.

She was beautiful and buffed to a shine, wearing what he imagined at a rough guess—Sam's wife, Nicole, would probably know the amount down to the dollar—to be about a hundred and fifty thousand dollars' worth of . . . stuff, from the designer purse, designer shoes, designer shades, to the big flashy designer jewels.

She'd carefully and slowly crossed her legs, showing a pantyless crotch that had been shaved except for a little landing strip in the middle, so she had a designer twat, too.

Harry *hated* this shit, but he had been designated by Sam and Mike as the go-to guy for the asshole clients, and he owed his two brothers so much he accepted the Asshole Detail without complaint.

Plus, they both knew that he was constitutionally incapable of being rude or discourteous to a woman.

His curse.

After quoting double their usual fee, Harry got the details, the copy of the tape of the delectable London fucking the man du jour, and the name and website of the so-called journalist who was going to post the tape tomorrow.

Five minutes after the door had closed behind London, Harry had found the file on the online tabloid's servers, degraded it, left some spyware and a very clear message that any attempt to post the file would cause the entire archives of the site to be degraded beyond repair, effectively putting them out of business. He toyed with the idea of signing the message "The Twat's Avenger" but decided not to. It was touch and go there for a moment, though.

Have to get your jollies where you can.

Five minutes, fifty thousand dollars. Not bad. And twenty-five thousand of that fifty was going into their Lost Ones Fund, their own personal Underground Railroad.

Twenty-five thousand dollars from London's trust fund would not be used to buy a fur or a week at a fancy spa or luxury rehab or a couple of Rolexes. That money would be spent on some abused woman who was running for her life. Most of the women who came to them left home under cover of darkness with nothing but the clothes on their backs, sometimes— tragically—with their kids. They did that because if they stayed they'd be beaten to death.

Harry and his brothers gave them a new life and enough money to start that life.

Great, great feeling. Maybe he should have charged London

triple their usual fee. Buy some safety for a lot of little kids, that would.

He was frowning over that when Marisa announced the next client, a Ms. Nora Charles.

She'd had an appointment with Sam, but Sam had called to say that Nicole was having bad morning sickness and he'd come in when she was better.

Harry knew his brother Sam. Not even the threat of nuclear war would keep Sam from Nicole's side when she wasn't feeling well. Sam would stay by her side until she felt better. That was the bottom line.

Harry respected that. He liked Nicole, a lot. And he liked it that she made Sam so happy. Well, happy . . . Sam seemed really happy with her when he wasn't panicking about some imaginary danger to Nicole around every corner. And now that there was a kid on the way, whoa.

Sam was going to have to dial down his crazy overprotectiveness, though Harry doubted he could. Sam Reston, big, huge, tough guy, good with a rifle, good with his fists, was a total wuss when it came to his wife. And the little girl on the way? Sam would probably keep her under armed guard throughout her childhood and let her date when she turned thirty. Maybe.

Mike was out on a recon for a jeweler who had received death threats.

So today Harry was it.

Nora Charles, huh? Did she think no one could remember the Thin Man movies? He sent up a little prayer. *Please, God, not another heiress under a fake name.* Harry had had his heiress quotient for the year with London even though it was still April.

He was bracing himself for more nonsense as his door slid open.

And then Marisa clicked twice on the intercom—their code—and he thought, *Oh shit.* Nora Charles had called on their special hotline, the underground railroad.

And then the most beautiful woman he'd ever seen walked in to his office.

Women were rarely clients of RBK Security, the mainstream, overground part of it, anyway. Mostly the clientele was corporate—something was leaking money and they wanted it stopped. Or they wanted their security system upgraded. He and Sam and Mike mostly dealt with their opposite corporate numbers, heads of security, or with the Big Guy himself—the CEO. Mostly men. And, of course, the odd heiress.

But the woman walking in to his office was definitely not an heiress. Not with those plain, nondescript clothes that were so rumpled they looked as if she'd slept in them. Not with those nails bitten down to the quick. Not with that glorious red hair tumbling wildly around her shoulders. Not with those dark circles under beautiful green eyes that were revealed when she pulled off her big sunglasses.

No, Harry thought sadly as he rose to greet her. She wasn't a pampered heiress. She was one of the Lost Ones.

CHAPTER 2

Ellen walked in to the office warily. Her friend Kerry had had dealings with the R of RBK, Sam Reston. So this was the B. Harry Bolt.

Kerry had talked about Sam Reston and hadn't said anything at all about the other two partners. Maybe Ellen was making a big mistake. Maybe this Bolt would turn her in to Gerald. Maybe she was signing her death warrant right now, she thought, as the door behind her slid silently closed, presenting a smooth expanse. She turned for a second, alarmed that the door had no doorknob and no hinges.

No way to get out.

It took her almost a full minute to realize that the button on the right-hand wall was probably the door release mechanism.

Heart pounding, Ellen turned back just as this Harry Bolt stood up. And up. And up.

He was amazingly tall. Amazingly . . . big. Huge, strong, unsmiling.

A lot of Gerald's operators had that look. Intent, focused, dangerous. Trained to hurt.

Ellen started to step back, but stopped herself. If there was one thing she'd learned in this past year, it was not to show fear. Her palms were sweating but she had no intention of shaking hands, so he didn't have to know.

"Ms. Charles? Please come in. Make yourself comfortable." Harry Bolt had a deep, calm voice. He watched her carefully, unmoving. Perhaps he realized that his size was unsettling and he did the only thing he could do to reassure her: stay still.

Heart thudding, Ellen walked carefully across the large office and sat down in one of two chairs facing his desk. Client chairs, clearly. If this was for real, if what Kerry had told her was true, and if this Harry Bolt did what Sam Reston did, then a lot of terrified women had sat in this very chair.

Were they all still alive? Had they been betrayed? Were they now rotting in some ditch or at the bottom of some lake, beaten to death?

Only one way to find out.

And yet she was so scared, it was hard to find enough oxygen to speak. She had to wait until she was certain that her voice would be strong and not shake.

This Harry Bolt didn't seem to have any problems with waiting. He'd taken his seat after her and just sat there, watching her.

His eyes were an extraordinary color. A light brown that looked almost golden, like an eagle's eyes. Ellen mentally shook herself. *Come on, you've got more important things to think about than the color of this guy's eyes. Like your life.*

She breathed in and out a few times, gathering her courage. Harry Bolt simply sat and waited, showing no signs of impatience.

Start obliquely, she thought. It would be a little test. If he had no idea what she was talking about, she'd go back outside and wait for Sam Reston, even if it took days.

Though she probably didn't have days. She might not live to see the sun set.

Deep breath. "The first thing I want to say is that Dove says hello. She says she's doing fine and she wants to thank you."

There. See what he made of that.

Harry Bolt watched her face intently, then nodded his head. "I'm glad," he said quietly, somberly. "Sam told me she's a good kid."

Right answer. Okay.

"Dove" was Kerry Robinson, and she *was* a good kid, but she'd had the bad luck to be married to a violent drunk who nearly killed her. Kerry Robinson wasn't her real name, and she'd known Ellen as Irene Ball. It didn't matter that their names weren't genuine because the danger to them was.

A year ago, Ellen had entered a world where women changed their names because there were monsters out looking for them. Somehow, Ellen had also entered some kind of sisterhood where not much had to be said to understand.

Some time back, Kerry had quietly told her that a man had been asking for her. It turned out he was only looking for a date, but Kerry had seen how scared Ellen was. And knew. So she'd given Ellen the special card with the special number on it that led to RBK.

"Are you in the same kind of trouble?" Harry Bolt asked quietly.

"Yes," she whispered.

"You're going to need to disappear?"

Among other things. "Yes."

He leaned forward slightly, resting his torso on muscled forearms. Ellen watched his hands carefully. They were large, scarred, powerful. He noted her glance and kept his hands very still.

She raised her eyes to his.

"I'm not the enemy," he said quietly.

Maybe. Maybe not.

She couldn't allow her vigilance to drop, not for one second. This man looked just as dangerous as any of Gerald's minions. More dangerous, even. He was perfectly able to repress those macho mess-with-me-and-you're-dead-meat vibes all of Gerald's men had, including Gerald himself.

This man was just as big and strong as the biggest and baddest of Gerald's men. And he'd been a Special Forces soldier. Ellen had read the thumbnail bios of all three partners in RBK at an Internet café, waiting for her appointment. She was going to place her life in the company's hands and she wanted to know what she was dealing with. So this Harry Bolt had been a Special Forces soldier and was way on top of the toughness scale, but his vibe was . . . calm. Serene.

Her intense anxiety went down half a notch.

They looked at each other, dead silence in the room.

Ellen was running possible openings through her mind when he said, voice still calm, "But you do have an enemy."

She nodded her head jerkily.

Oh God, this was so *hard*.

"Why don't you start at the beginning?" he suggested.

She drew in a deep breath. Beginning. Okay.

"I, um. I'm an accountant. A CPA." She thought about it, about the smoking ruins of her existence. "Or was. In another life."

LISA MARIE RICE is eternally 30 years old and will never age. She is tall and willowy and beautiful. Men drop at her feet like ripe pears. She has won every major book prize in the world. She is a black belt with advanced degrees in archeology, nuclear physics and Tibetan literature. She is a concert pianist. Did I mention the Nobel? Of course, Lisa Marie Rice is a virtual woman and exists only at the keyboard when writing erotic romance. She disappears when the monitor winks off.

Be Impulsive!

Look for Other
Avon Impulse Authors

www.AvonImpulse.com